1

1

My head was pounding, and my skin felt like it was on fire. Opening my eyes didn't help a thing, and my stomach was like an ocean, sloshing this way and that, threatening to expel its contents.

I didn't know if it was from the drinking or my husband. Either way, today was another dreadful day. Maybe Edward would join my previous two husbands in the cemetery before long.

Wouldn't that be another lucky break? I thought ruefully. Said husband unceremoniously shoved me, my cue to get breakfast started.

I really ought to poison it this time, I thought. Everyone thought I did anyway; what difference would it make?

Not much for talking, Edward tended to use his brawn over his brains. I was told what to do and when with shoves and kicks, fists when necessary.

At this point, I didn't care. It was better than Samuel's incessant chatter.

Miserable man that he was, he had to make everyone around him sad, too. He would go on and on about how horrible I was, how bad the weather was, and what a lousy house we had. If I didn't know any better, I would think the chicken bone he choked on was the chicken telling him to shut up. It worked.

And before then was Thomas. Poor, stupid Thomas. Now that one did ask for it. Thomas would pick a fight with a blade of grass if he thought it jabbed him on purpose.

I would have felt more sympathy if he weren't so rotten. Cruelty was his armor, like his father before him. Just mean to the bone, but he had a smile that could light up the room.

And a laugh; he loved to laugh whether he was happy or sad. He'd beat me within an inch of my life, laughing all the while.

Until he was beaten to death, that is. I always told him to pick a fight with someone his size. And guess what? He lost.

No, I was lucky to have Edward. A widow like me? Oh boy, I was sure lucky to find a man who would marry a woman twice widowed. Yeah, sure, and so is the cow when it's his turn for slaughter.

I'd rather be the cow.

But a woman can't be without a man, can she? Why, who would keep her in line? Especially a woman like me, spending my evenings in the tavern to escape my rotten husbands.

No wonder I was beaten bloody, they'd say, over their cups of ale. Awful lot they were, too.

"Bridget," Edward said as he shoved me again, much harder this time.

Narrowly escaping smashing my head on the side table, I strode out of bed to the kitchen. At least my husband had money, I thought as I made us a breakfast of porridge.

Sitting down at the table to stem the spins that overtook me, I marveled at a raven perched on the windowsill. Maybe he would peck Edward's eyes out, I thought.

————————-

"Bridget!" Edward screamed from the bedroom.

Shit, I must have dozed while the food cooked. Hurrying to the stove, it was remarkably well done.

"Coming!" I shouted back.

I guess this meant his eyes were intact. Maybe it's my fault I have such terrible husbands; what a horrible wife I am. Cursing at myself in my head, I scooped the porridge into bowls. How could I fall asleep making breakfast?

Maybe God was punishing me for my lack of appreciation for the multitude of husbands He'd sent. Or the amount of liquor still coursing through my body.

If I were going to Hell, I would do it my way, at least.

Stumbling into the bedroom, I served my lazy slob of a husband as a good wife should. I even averted my eyes, so he didn't have to see the disgust I felt for him.

He smacked my thigh, hurrying me on like a horse. As I ate, I dressed, and cleaned the mess I had made making breakfast. Porridge slopped down the side of the pot, pooled where I had poured it into the bowls. I was thankful I was able to choke most of my food down.

Edward left without a word, leaving me to my tasks. Clean this, mend that, tend the meager vegetables we grow, feed the animals, clean their pens. It was always the same.

My father thought I should be appreciative I have had the good fortune to have such well-to-do husbands. He can pick winners, he tells me. I'm not sure if he ever notices the bruises. If he does, he doesn't seem to mind—self-centered ass.

But he is my father all the same.

I'm their property, like the horse or the house, no different. Resigned to my fate, I started about my day, regretting eating anything.

The morning sun was already too warm for my liking, with a promise to only get hotter. A dragonfly landed on my arm for a moment before flitting off to do whatever it was they did. It was early June, and the summer ahead was starting to seem like a hot one.

Maybe today would be all right. At least Edward was gone all day.

He wasn't that horrible, sure. He hit, but mostly they were solid thwacks. There was no warmth to be had, but there was no malice either. Our marriage was an exchange. He needed an obedient wife, and I needed a husband to keep me in line. I was often out of line is the problem.

With Samuel, it was constant complaining, constant hits, constant blaming. If the weather was dreary, it was my fault. When he had a headache, it was my fault. Everything was always my fault.

Thomas was different. His cruelty had seeped into my bones until it became a part of me. Warmth he had, but it was the warmth that destroyed a person. It was the way he lured you in with his charisma before he abused you that did it.

He could make me feel feelings I didn't know existed, maybe even love. And then he would use it against you. Take those feelings and make you regret ever having them.

It was the same in town. He would make friends with anybody before tearing them down. With his smile and his banter, he had a handsome face that he used well. Trick you into thinking maybe he wasn't so bad.

Until he was.

He got what he deserved in the end, I guess. But I'd be lying if I said I never missed him. Masochistic, I know.

Last night was a night like any other. Edward was a sawyer, so we'd be in town often for different contracts for the townspeople. We went to town to discuss what he would saw up next. What kind of lumber, where, for what? A lot of those deals happened in the tavern.

I was not supposed to drink when we went to do business. I was never supposed to drink. Especially not with how it makes me behave, according to my husband.

That's what Edward was telling me as he used his fists to make his point last night when we got home. What a disgrace I was, what a terrible wife. No wonder he was my third husband.

I was quite past the point of caring. So while he made his contracts, I would drink. He couldn't beat me in public, anyway. Plus, the alcohol numbed the pain.

All of it.

And as always, he would usher me home to dole out my punishment behind closed doors. Even on the nights I didn't drink. It would be the way I looked at the wait staff or how I looked bored.

Edward was the oldest of my husbands, a widower himself. His previous wife probably died due to lack of excitement, her poor heart just wasting away.

The raven was perched on the periphery of our land, standing on a fence post. It caught my attention and shouted at me in its raven way, the loud ca-caw making my aching head protest. The bird seemed mildly amused by my wince and did it again like we were in conversation.

I was not amused.

As the day wore on, my headache subsided, but I was lightheaded. I was in the kitchen making lunch when the bird caught my attention again. It had left its post on the fence to stand by the well and screech some more, reminding me that I had not had a drink of water all day.

Rolling my eyes at the bird, I poured myself some water from the pitcher we kept in the house. I would need to fetch more before Edward made it home, or I was asking for another beating.

Returning my attention to the well, the bird was gone, and so was most of the day. If I didn't pick up my pace, I would be asking for a beating because I didn't finish my chores.

I ate my lunch ruefully, imagining flying away like the bird.

By the time Edward returned, I had finished my chores by the skin of my teeth. My heart beat painfully from the pace I had pushed through the second half of the day.

I made a meager stew meal for supper, knowing he wouldn't be pleased, but it was the only way to cook the items we had, near spoiled as they were.

He hit me for my carelessness, letting the food get so close to spoiling. And a shove for making stew on a hot day such as this. But he ate it without complaint, at least.

I had little appetite after the hot day. My stomach still felt like it was filled with the porridge from this morning and the liquor last night. So while he ate, I moved my food around with my fork, staring out the window in silence.

The raven was there again, standing on the well. I remembered to drink some water. He cawed loudly, and I nibbled at my bread while I stared at the odd creature. Ravens were more intelligent than the rest of their kind. This one was no exception.

I think it spoke to me more than my husband.

"Bridget," Edward said on cue.

It was probably the only thing I heard him say to me, "Bridget." Concisely said without inflection. It was an order and a curse in one word.

This time the order was that he was finished with his dinner, and I ought to clean up. He wouldn't repeat my name.

Having finished most of my bread, I got up to clean, tossing my stew to the pigs. I smiled at the raven. He had come to join me near the pen. I gave him the rest of my bread.

It felt nice to have a friend.

"Are you lonely too?" I asked him.

It seemed a like him.

He gave me the typical bird look, head sideways for a moment before eating his bread. I laughed out loud. I had almost expected him to answer, as he had been to this point. How absurd.

My peal of laughter startled me, so unused to it at this point. The bird gave me another look, and I laughed again, reveling in the feel of it.

A tightness I didn't know existed loosened in my chest a little, just for a moment. But it was enough, a brief respite before sadness washed over me again. I couldn't afford lightness. It was a feeling reserved for godly people, not someone like me.

Giving the bird one last smile, I thanked him for his gift. He cawed in response, and I felt a little less lonely before I headed back inside.

CHAPTER 2

Declan glared at me as I entered the dining room, where we had all just been gathered.

"What are you doing back? I thought you were leaving. Where's Bridget?" Declan said, confusion and worry quickly clouding his features.

Damn it if this wasn't the worst type of punishment.

"The Queen of Elphame has her," I said, knowing it in my bones.

"What the hell are you talking about, Ruad? I thought you said we had time? What do you mean she has her? Where?" Declan said, his fair skin turning scarlet in the blink of an eye.

"Where? In her world, I thought we had time, but I was mistaken."

"Aren't you bloody supposed to know everything?" he roared. "What good are you if you're mistaken half the time and the other half you can't tell us what to do next?"

He finished the last with a fist slammed on the table. He wasn't wrong, but that wasn't the way it worked, much to everyone's dismay.

"They're cycles, they have patterns, but I don't know specifically all the time what cycle it is. Or when the next thing will happen, or how, I have a strong intuition is all it boils down to really."

"Bloody useless power, if you ask me," he spat.

I agreed.

"I love her too, don't forget. But this is one of the things she needs to do herself. If she doesn't this time, it will only show up again later. That's the nature of cycles. She has to break it."

He cracked his neck with a quick turn of his head before visibly softening at that one. Like he had to release the anger in the shake of his head.

That's what made this the worst. He was hard to hate. Even if everything in me wanted to.

"Right, fine. So what are we supposed to do?"

"Well, that depends. For now, I'm working on reaching her in the world she's in, trying to guide her back to our world. You need to work on finding her physical body."

"How? How are you guiding her back? How the hell am I supposed to find her? How the hell did she get her?" the frustration was back as quickly as it had left.

"The queen's power is like Darkness's, in the way he could manipulate a person's reality. Where Darkness would bring your mind into his world, and all was black and empty, the queen is most powerful when she gets a person into her realm. Where her magic reigns supreme. She traps a person in this virtual reality, and she can create anything she chooses for the person.

"So, while Bridget believes that the world she is in is real, she is only experiencing a reality the queen has chosen for her."

"But what of *her?* Is she walking and talking in this reality?"

"Her physical body could be interacting in this reality in her mind, but I find it unlikely. You need space for that, and then you wouldn't want them to trip and break the spell. So it's likely the queen has her sedentary somewhere in the Otherworld."

"How did she get her, though? We were both right here."

"The queen has the ability to manipulate people. She has limitations, of course, but she was able to magic Bridget away, likely through someone else. Similar to Nick being manipulated by Evil."

"By who? You?" Declan snapped.

"Your anger is justified, but no, not me."

His eyes went vacant as he tallied the events of the morning.

"Loretta…" Declan said as he turned on his heel and stalked away.

I was a step behind as he crashed into the kitchen with authority.

Loretta was standing at the sink, cleaning the remnants of the meal we had shared. She jumped in alarm at the intrusion.

"Loretta, where's Bridget?" Declan asked.

"She was with you. What do you mean?"

"Do you remember when you saw her last?"

"Well, I was cleaning up, and she was walking your guest to the door…" Her face scrunched in confusion.

"Loretta, what do you remember after that?"

"I don't remember anything after that. I'd brought the dishes to be cleaned, and I suppose I started cleaning them…" She trailed off again in confusion.

"Are you missing a chunk of time?" I chimed in.

"I…" She glanced at the time before continuing. "The last I knew, I was carrying the plates in, and it was just after ten, so I was planning on asking Declan if they wanted a light lunch or a late lunch. But it's nearing eleven now, and I don't know why I've only started the dishes. It shouldn't have taken that long."

Declan looked at me for help. I gave him a shrug. He knew Loretta better than me. He could be the one to fill her in or not. He made up his mind and grabbed Loretta's hand to sit her down, and I excused myself to see if there were any clues the queen may have left behind.

I was examining the doorway and the lack of protection around it when Declan rejoined me. The warding was gone, so the queen likely got to Loretta and made sure she eliminated the herbs. Quickly remedying that, I enhanced the protection throughout the house with a trickier spell.

I nearly passed out from the effort.

"How is she?" I asked.

"She'll be fine. She's as superstitious as my mother, so she's not even entirely surprised. Said she could tell you were different." He said the last with an eye roll. "To be quite honest, it's my mother I'm worried about. She'll think the whole mess is her fault for meddling as she did."

"Well, you'll find out soon enough. She's who you have to call."

"What does my mother have to do with this?"

"There's warding blocking me from seeing her location. Your mother will know how to find Bridget the fastest. I can locate her eventually, but I would need her to wake up. Currently, she's still unaware she's under a spell."

"And how is it that you're communicating with her?"

"The queen's realm is my realm, where I go when I'm not needed here, like Asgard. We call it the Otherworld, and while it's all interconnected, we each have our own space. The queen is among the more powerful of the Gods and Goddesses, and her space is better protected against outsiders because she doesn't like to play nicely amongst us all,

"But due to my connection to Bridget..." His lips thinned at that one. "I can speak to her through her subconscious. Spiritually, I am tethered to her, and it's through that connection that I'm able to send her messages in the Otherworld. Though technically, I can get into any of your heads if I want, Bridget and I have a stronger line of communication,"

He ignored that one.

"Can you see how she is? What's happening in the Otherworld?"

"She's fine, as she always is. This is a rather unsavory past life of hers that the queen is having her play out. Currently, I'm sending her signs in the animals she interacts with and speaking to her through a raven, the animal she and I are most closely associated with."

"What past life? Is she hurt? Are you using actual words?"

His concern kept showing in the multitude of questions he threw at me. A man used to having the answers, not asking the questions.

"No, no words, but Bridget is always in tune with the spirit world. She knows there's something special about the bird, but she doesn't know why yet. That's my job, to help her awaken from the dream the queen has her in. If I can do that, I can locate her and get her out of there.

"And she's not hurt, per se," I said with a sigh. "In real life, the queen can keep her alive indefinitely if she chooses, making her bait for you, who she wants. So, that's a good reason to believe her physical body will remain intact for now. Almost as if she's frozen in time…"

I halted at that, hesitating.

"Continue."

I hated saying it aloud. It was like admitting it was real.

"In the Otherworld, her physical body is not being harmed, but to her, it is. She's essentially dreaming, but to her, it's reality. She has no recollection of this life or that there is a different life. The world she's stuck in is one of my least favorite."

Declan was growing impatient. His body was vibrating with anger that reflected mine.

"This is the one where she is hanged,"

CHAPTER 3

I awoke in the dark, confused and still very tired. It was late, and I wasn't sure why I was awake until I heard Edward's groans.

"Are you well?" I asked him.

He only groaned in response, hunched over, sitting next to me in bed. Sitting up, I leaned over until I could see his face.

Pale and sweaty, he still managed to glare at me before he backhanded me.

"Bridget," he spat, an admonishment.

"What can I do for you, husband?" I said.

I may have spat the husband part at him. But I was a good wife, right?

"Water," was all he said.

So he does know more words, I thought spitefully. Fetching the water, I was half expecting to see the raven.

Sighing inwardly at his absence, I brought Edward the water. My only companion is a bird, I thought as I handed him the glass.

He took a few shaky sips before shoving the glass at me and expelling the contents of his stomach all over the floor. That woke me up significantly, and I began to worry.

"Edward, here, drink more water," I said, shoving the glass into his hands.

He swatted it away, grabbing my wrist instead and grasping it cruelly. Pulling me towards him, forcing me to stand in his sickness, he smacked me with his free hand.

"Was this you? Thought you'd poison me finally?"

"What? Edward, no! You've fallen ill, is all. This will pass."

"You'd better hope it does. There will be no fourth husband waiting for you,"

I was terrified he was right.

Three were already too many. As it was, people whispered about me in town. If only they knew the whole of it. Not that they'd believe me if I tried to tell them.

Releasing my wrist, he shoved me away from him. Taking my cue, I went and got a bucket and some clothes to clean the mess he had made, tracking it through the house with me.

Heading outside for freshwater, I was delighted to be out of the stench and suffocating air from inside. The air was beautiful; a cool breeze rustled the leaves, the humidity of the day gone with it. Checking my surroundings, my delight was dampened slightly by the continued lack of the raven.

I knew the bird was most likely sleeping, but I sincerely hoped it would return come morning. The comfort I took in his presence was silly, I knew, but it was a comfort all the same. Something I was sorely lacking in life.

As I cleaned, Edward returned to a night of fitful sleep, and I was glad to escape his scrutiny. Lost in thought, I kept wondering how I had come to this—scrubbing the floor in the middle of the night with my third abusive husband sleeping nearby.

Samuel was my first husband, a marriage of social stature. Older and still unmarried, Samuel needed a wife. His social status was much higher than mine. It was a perfect marriage for me and satisfactory for him.

I quickly learned his lack of a wife was due to his disagreeable personality. Nothing made the man happy.

Wide-eyed and innocent, I had taken my duty as a wife with the utmost sincerity, only to be met with constant criticism. The verbal reprimands became physical until I was neither wide-eyed nor innocent, but still, I maintained my integrity and gave the marriage my all.

His death seemed a blessing to me. God was finally smiling at me, I had thought.

And when I met Thomas, I thought it was God's plan all along.

Thomas was handsome and charming. He swept me off my feet with his generosity. What a wonderful man to marry a widow, I thought.

Our courtship was one of wonder and romance. He was forever making thoughtful gestures to woo me. It was a marriage of love, at first.

When the cruelty began, I would constantly excuse his behavior. He was having a bad day. The weather had him down. I needed to try harder.

Then the rumors began to circulate. Thomas would be seen with other women in town under questionable circumstances. And still, I made excuses for him. He was my husband after all, and he married me because he loved me.

Then the drinking began to grow out of control. There were no more romantic gestures, only lewd remarks and angry outbursts. As if my duty as a wife was only to obey him.

Even after his death, I struggled to match the man I married with the one I was married to. His behavior had grown increasingly erratic and outlandish as the years went on that I still couldn't maintain that was not who he was, only a product of my inability to keep him happy.

He had suffered at the hands of another man in town, a man whose wife it was rumored that Thomas had been seen with. That was ultimately what had driven me to Edward.

Dependable Edward, severe Edward, dogmatic Edward, he was the polar opposite of Thomas, which I liked about him. He was harsh and could be cruel, but it wasn't always unjustified.

16

I wasn't the girl I used to be.

Gone were the wide eyes and innocence. I wasn't the wife that longed to be good and obedient anymore. They can all rot in hell.

Just not too soon, I hoped. Edward was severe, but I would take him over what next fresh hell I might be in for if he died.

Blanching at that, I almost lost the contents of my stomach. The devil I knew was better than the one I didn't.

Finally finished cleaning, it was near dawn, and I was filthy. Deciding to bathe before I started the day, I went outside to dump the contents of my pail and rinse off in the stream.

The raven met me at the door, and a thrill went through me. If things didn't go well with Edward, maybe I could run away with the bird. I rolled my eyes at myself. How pitiful was I?

Don't be absurd. You're just lonely and tired. Any other person in your position would befriend a bird, too.

At least, that's what I said in my head to soothe myself.

"Well, good morning. Did you sleep well?" I asked him.

It was only polite, and it comforted me. What could it hurt?

He cocked his head to the side and gave a small squawk. I took that as a yes.

Dumping the pail, I headed back to the house to grab a piece of bread for him. If we kept up our friendship, I would have to bake more bread. It was a small price to pay for a friend, in my opinion.

I used to have a few real ones, but I'm afraid Thomas was the one that swiftly ended those. At first it was little things he didn't like about them. They were too chatty; they weren't polished enough.

Then it was challenging to explain the rumors to them and keep Thomas away from their prying eyes.

And then there were the bruises.

Thomas had systematically isolated me from them before I knew it. Then, I would go to town and watch them cross the street to avoid me.

When Thomas was gone, I tried to reconnect with a few of the women I had been close with, but it was never the same. They knew I kept secrets from them, and they felt they couldn't trust me.

And maybe they were right.

When Thomas was alive, I was afraid of his retribution if I spoke up and afraid no one would believe me, regardless. And when he was gone, I didn't want to speak ill of the dead. Only in my head, I was allowed to do that, not out loud.

And so, the women no longer trusted me. It was understandable.

Then when I married again, Edward moved us further from the town. He liked his solitude, and the city held nothing for me anymore. So we went for business, and I was friendly, but I had no more friends.

The women I used to socialize with talked behind their hands when I was around, and I tried to smile and be polite as I drank more ale. I found that I cared a lot less the more I drank, so why stop?

A few women were still friendly, but then the hand talkers just turned their attention to those women. So, for the sake of the familiar faces, I tried to avoid them. They didn't need to join me in exile.

Exile was small comfort to me, relinquished from the necessity of conjuring up more excuses. Edward took more care in his heavy hand, but all the same, there were occasional bruises. It was my skin tone. It showed all.

It felt better to be alone than to continue to lie to the people that may have cared for me. Like borrowing someone else's coat, their kindness was warm, but it wasn't mine to keep.

18

Returning it and forgetting about it seemed the kindest way to be.

A few weren't outwardly cruel, but many were. Some of them smiled at me, but not much more, like Mary. She always had a warm greeting for me.

Maybe the only one, but I appreciated it.

Feeding the raven, I thought I ought to call him something. If he was a friend, he should have a name.

"What should I call you?" I asked him.

He took his bread and landed on the little deck to eat it. Something tingled in my brain, a memory forgotten; I got the faint impression I knew this bird in another life. The familiarity was so uncanny.

Names held power, I remembered. I could settle for just calling him "bird" for now.

I peeled off my filthy clothes and went to the stream near the house. The water was pleasant in the warm air, and I nearly moaned in ecstasy from it.

The water soothed my aching muscles as much as my aching soul, and I allowed it to clear away everything. All of my thoughts, pain, and worries floated downriver until I felt nearly whole again.

Nearly.

I would have liked to stay here all day, naked as the day I was born, and let the sunshine warm the parts of me long gone cold. As it was, the ice around my heart floated away, carried on the wind as a gentle breeze blew.

There was a time I wasn't so guarded. Maybe never carefree, but a little more open to the world and its possibilities.

I couldn't afford that anymore. Only in these brief moments alone would I allow myself to relax.

Well, just me and the bird.

I peeked over at him, still eating his bread. He looked at me when he noticed my attention, and I laughed a little. What an odd bird.

Thinking I was losing the time allowed, I got up to start the day before Edward woke up and yelled at me for my laziness. As if bathing were frivolous and unnecessary.

With the beginnings of a massive headache, I yearned for something to drink. But Edward, in his severity, had no use for any alcohol in the house, much to my dismay.

Unlike Thomas, Edward wasn't much for drink. His austerity was Godliness, in his opinion. Drink hindered that.

I wasn't sure how God felt about hitting your wife, but who was I to question? Indeed, I wasn't headed to Heaven when my day came.

The headache, the lack of food, and the sleepless night left me very weak and irritable, and I wanted so desperately to have a hot breakfast this instant, but I had to cook it first. Instead, I grabbed some of the bread I had set aside for the bird and ate it. He just stared at me.

"Sorry bird, I was going to give this to you, but I'm famished," I said to him.

To my astonishment, he nudged a piece of bread untouched toward me with his beak. I knew these birds were intelligent, but there was something different about his gaze I couldn't get over.

I might tease myself, saying that he seems familiar to me, but the pushing bread to me was...extraordinary. Alarm bells were going off in my head, and still, I stared at the bird. My brain was trying to tell me something I couldn't grasp.

Or I was severely depleted and possibly hallucinating.

Tentatively, I reached out to touch the birds' feathers, uncertainty making my stomach tighten. With my luck, it was just a rabid bird, and he'd peck *my* eyes out. But something told me he wouldn't.

As my hand inched closer, the bird turned into it, rubbing his head against my outstretched hand as any friendly animal would. Taking my cue, I moved my body just a touch closer so I could better pet him.

There was such a sense of peace you get when sharing something simple like this with another living thing. That calmness fills the void inside of you. It quiets the rage that always seems to be there, festering.

At least for me.

The bird seemed to agree with me, and he pushed more firmly into my hand. I resisted the urge to pick him up and hug him to me, certain that would be what made him turn on me.

It just felt so lovely to be...loved. If that's what I could call this.

Such a simple gesture in a cold world, love. Sharing kindness with a like-minded individual for the sake of spreading your light. Giving instead of taking.

I used to be that way. That was a different world, though.

Melting into his touch I noticed that his feathers weren't pitch black like I thought they were. This close they were more like a dark bronze in the sun, so shiny it looked like it glowed.

I couldn't shake the sense that I was missing something. But more likely, I was just trying to will something into reality that wasn't true. A meaning greater than what existed.

It was easy to get carried away. And dangerous. No one was coming to save me, especially not a bird. Not even a smart and sweet one like this guy.

The magic of the moment broken I realized there were tears in my eyes. Poor little guy must feel like I do. At least he had wings.

"Thank you for that," I whispered to him, not able to speak much louder than a whisper.

He looked at me with piercing beady little eyes and I swear he looked as heartbroken as I felt. Or maybe I had officially gone off the deep end.

"Bridget!" Edward roared from the bedroom.

I jumped out of my skin, letting out a shriek as I did so. I'd been too caught up in the bird. To my never-ending surprise the bird did not react to my outburst. He just continued to look at me quizzically.

"Go on now, bird. Fly away before you can't," I whispered.

If only someone had given me the same advice.

It hurt to leave my only friend though and before I scurried off, I gave him a gentle hug against my chest. He snuggled in, and I savored the feel of a gentle soul so close to me. For whatever reason he made me immeasurably happy, and I was grateful for it, if perplexed.

Making my way inside, I saw Edward in the doorway, pale and shaky. His face was twisted in disapproval.

"What are you about woman?" he spat at me.

"I was bathing Edward. I was filthy," I said with the least amount of venom I could muster.

"Was that a bird you were holding just now?"

Shit.

"Yes. He's a lonely old fellow it seems. He's been hanging around lately and he likes my company."

At least someone fucking does.

Edward would've smacked me right then and there if I cursed in front of him. Unladylike he says. Fuck him.

"Get rid of it. Filthy creatures."

You're a filthy creature.

"Fine," was all I said.

"Where's my food?"

"What would you like?"

"What do you think I want? Are you just trying to be difficult this morning?"

Whack.

He had crossed the room in two strides and backhanded me. I suppose I *was* trying to be difficult this morning.

Sick or not his backhand had force behind it and tiny black spots danced across my eyes for a few moments. I wouldn't let him have the satisfaction though, so I started on breakfast. Porridge, always porridge with him.

Thomas used to like variety, and always ale or cider at breakfast. Everything with him was excess, and with Edward everything was minimal. And Samuel it didn't fucking matter. He was miserable no matter what you gave him.

When my vision cleared enough to look up again I saw the bird still there. Somehow having a witness to my shame was even worse than suffering alone.

I gave him a small smile and a wave of my hand. Silly bird seemed so lonely to be sitting around hanging out with me, watching me through the window.

I may not like him witnessing my outright abuse but now that Edward had retreated back to the bedroom it was nice to have company. He hopped on over to the well to stare at me from there and I remembered to drink more water. Useful bird he was.

Once breakfast was finished and Edward had eaten a few morsels, he told me to go into town to get him the antidote to whatever I had poisoned him with. I didn't let him see me roll my eyes nor did I acknowledge the poisoning jab, but I conceded.

Truthfully I was glad to be headed to town. Anywhere away from here was nice for a change.

After getting myself ready to go I headed out to saddle the horse. To my dismay the bird was gone, but I had a feeling he would be back.

And that was enough for me.

CHAPTER 4

"You're really going to want to elaborate, Ruad," Declan said in a voice that brooked no argument.

He was a worthy adversary, if that's what he was, anyway.

"The queen isn't stupid. Mad, yes, but an idiot, no. Naturally she chose the worst life Bridget has led, to date at least. She's in Salem and she will be the first of many to be hanged for witchcraft. The true genius behind the madness is that it is me that will be the last nail in her coffin."

"How?" Declan's voice was thick with emotions.

"I'm trying to wake her up, but I can hardly go waltzing up to her. This isn't one I'm able to, it would only make it worse. So I'm using my other form, a raven,"

"And witches are associated with ravens."

"Now, yes."

"Are you saying you're responsible for that?"

"I'm not the only supernatural being that can take the form of a raven. But I suppose I didn't help things."

"So how do you condemn her?"

"This Bridget has had a series of unfortunate events occur. Her third husband will die soon like her first two did, and she will be accused of witchcraft and hanged. She was obviously not responsible for the deaths of her husbands, but it was the way a raven seemed to talk to her that eventually was the tipping point."

"And so what? You do nothing? What if she never wakes up?"

"Waking up isn't enough. We still need to find her. Unfortunately, I believe this means that the queen is doing this to directly toy with me. The positive side is that the queen wants you, not Bridget. I think that even if we don't get her to wake up in this life, she will just be put into another one. The queen will keep her alive as long as she is useful."

"But she'll die soon?" Declan said, the color in his face rising belying the intensity of his emotions.

"Yes," I said.

The statement hung in the air, neither of us looking at the other.

I was used to losing Bridget. But it never hurt any less. Declan was sorting through a similar range of emotions, except this was the first time for him. While sympathetic, every second the clock ticked was another second Bridget was stuck in her own personal hell.

"So what do we do?" Declan broke the silence first.

"We really don't have a choice do we? I have to keep trying even if it damns her. And you still need to get your mother here."

There was another pause before he spoke again.

"How bad is it?" he whispered.

I opened my mouth, but nothing came out. Blowing out a breath I didn't realize I'd been holding I gave him a small shake of my head.

"Nothing she can't handle. But it's not good. Her husbands earned their early graves," I said by way of explanation.

"Nothing she can't handle," he whispered solemnly.

It wasn't a good feeling. Not being able to help. Knowing that by helping we were only hurting her more.

Because when we did find her, we were putting Declan at risk. And my trying to help her was going to kill her.

"That's why you can't go in as you," he said.

"She's been through enough already. Her latest husband has kept her isolated. A strange man knocking on the door wouldn't be met with understanding."

"Right."

He was battling his desire to go in guns blazing and I understood the frustration. Walking over to the fireplace he leaned his hands on the mantle and hung his head a minute.

"I have an opportunity. She needs to go into the town to get medicine. Her husband is already sick. But I'm afraid it won't make a difference; she's pretty far removed in this life," I said softly.

"Do it, I'll call my mother," he said, head still hung.

I took that as my cue to leave and I walked out the front door for the fresh air. There was a suffocating feeling that wasn't budging, and nature was usually the only thing that helped. There was time yet for Bridget to get to town and Joan to get here.

So much had happened in such a short period I needed to clear my head so I could think straight, so I headed for the woods.

It was a bit of a walk, but I knew Declan needed the space before his mother arrived. I wasn't sure who Joan may be descended from, but it was clear she was special.

As I walked, I contemplated on the events of the past week. It didn't seem possible, but it was only days ago that I first met with Declan and Bridget in the woods I was walking toward now.

My heart dropped into my stomach, thinking of seeing her for the first time again. It had been too long this time.

I ended that thought before it could begin.

I knew it before I saw him, a change in the atmosphere, that intuitive knowing you get when you're aligned with the world around you. Everything spoke if you were willing to listen.

Turning my head slightly to the left, I saw him then, standing amongst a copse of trees, jutted out to hug the water's edge. Dagda.

He was tall and broad, with silver hair and beard, and dark eyes as hard as flint. His cloak rippled in the breeze, and he was clutching his staff in one hand. And he was Brigid's father.

The epitome of masculinity he had work-hardened muscles, square jaw, and a formidable presence. His being here couldn't be good news.

I inclined my head in greeting. We knew each other well.

"Ruad," he said as he inclined his head back.

"Dagda, I wasn't anticipating you," I said a little terser than I had expected to.

"Nor I you. How is it do you suppose you find me here?"

Well, he didn't have to be rude.

"Yes, Bridget, the queen, understood. But I didn't think it was so serious as to bring you here."

We had a comfortable if not a warm relationship. I was a part of his counsel. Being all-knowing I was useful. And if I was being honest, he was a good man and a good leader. There were just a few things we disagreed upon. A few major things.

"I also suppose you know what my presence means."

It meant this was a *really* shitty cycle we were in.

"Suppose I do."

He usually called when he needed me. But that he was calling on me now was ominous.

"The queen needs Lugh, this Declan, to secure her hold. She's planning a coup for control of Brú Na Bóinne and the Otherworld."

Which meant we were going to lose.

———

When I returned to the house Joan was already there as evidenced by the car in the driveway. After my conversation with Dagda, I wasn't in a rush to get back.

There wasn't a good way to tell Declan what was likely to happen next, and I wasn't sure I was going to. If it was inevitable, I was only causing him more grief.

Either way with Joan present I wasn't broaching the subject just now. Finding Bridget was still the primary objective. The rest would unfold regardless.

I hadn't met Joan officially but from Bridget's feelings of her, I knew she was kind. And any parent of the Dál gCais were usually cut from the same cloth even if they themselves weren't direct descendants. I estimated that it was Joan that was a descendant of the original clan, knowing his surname. I wondered what Joan's maiden name was. Though if I had to guess it was likely O'Brien.

Declan came from an impressive pedigree. Two formidable clans with high rank. Both clans were kings in their day. It wasn't a surprise that Declan was a reincarnation of Lugh himself.

Even if it did grate a little.

I was a fan of Lugh, it was hard not to be. We usually were on the same side of things, not opposing. Though I guess that was the case here as well, with one significant wedge between us.

Walking in the front door, it was apparent that Declan had apprised them of the predicament. By the furrow of his father's brow, he had informed them of my *investment* with Bridget as well.

They were all smiles though and willing to embrace my presence even if they were wary. People got uncomfortable around Gods, it was understandable.

I couldn't exactly read minds, but I could see more than the average human. Joan excluded, she wasn't average.

She was the first to approach me and embraced me before I had a chance to prepare. Not unexpected, considering her lineage. I wrapped tender arms around her to appease all parties.

Humans years ago worshipped us, none more than the Dál gCais. The wariness on her husband's face was one of a man worried for his wife. The look in her eyes was warmth and a little bit of reverence.

"Nice to meet you as well, Joan," I said as I looked into her eyes.

Glancing at Declan's father I inclined my head in welcome. "Brian," I said.

He inclined his back, and that was that.

Joan was still entranced, staring intensely at me to the point that both men began to fidget. She ignored them and took a slow walk around me, much to my amusement.

The smile that took over my face surprised even me, but I was enamored with her too. So brazen. It's not a surprise Declan fell for Bridget. Both women had such spirit.

"So you're a God?" she said almost flippantly.

"Are you disappointed?" I said with a laugh.

I felt like an exhibit at the zoo. She didn't mean it rudely though, only reassuring that she had the facts straight. It wasn't something I was unused to, but it had been a long time since we were worshipped openly.

"I wouldn't say that," she said.

I smiled and gave her a wink.

"Bridget's a lucky girl that's all I'll say. Well, despite her current state of affairs," she said before addressing the room. "Now how are we going to get our girl?"

Ogling aside we were to the heart of the matter and the air felt like it was knocked out of my lungs. Declan spared me and answered his mother's question while I composed myself, giving me a querying look.

"We need a spell or a divination to find her, I imagine. We thought you would be able to help us," he said.

"Yes, that's precisely what I was thinking. I need the book I had given her. Do you know where it is?" she asked Declan.

He looked at me. I knew where it was too, in the library. I nodded and set out to fetch it, grateful for his thoughtfulness in giving me a moment to compose myself. And only slightly annoyed that he was so difficult to dislike.

Returning with the book in hand, I saw that Joan already had a book from the shelves lining this room open and was sorting through the likely suspects. Opening to a map, she unclasped her necklace and set it down before putting her hands out for the book.

"It's a simple spell really. I'll need someone to hold the book while I recite the words and the charm on my necklace should point us in her direction," she said.

There were thousands of ways to find someone supernaturally. I was proud of her efficiency.

I tuned into her frequency for a moment as the raven and found that she was still preparing for her trip to town. She was feeding the horse that would take her.

I hadn't told Declan yet that I'd sent Failinis to be my eyes when I wasn't there. I'd done it as soon as I knew she was going to town. Enbarr was still here to keep watch over Declan, but the dog was likely sleeping since I was here.

The queen was unlikely to notice the horse that Bridget was riding. And unlikely to attack here while she knew I was here.

I was grateful because we ought to have her location soon and I would be able to go as myself when she was in town. But I was happy the queen didn't think to try any funny business like speeding up the time yet.

Otherworld was where magic reigned supreme. The queen could do as she pleased with someone she could capture and take there.

Back in the present, Brian was holding the book for Joan while she held the necklace over the map. The pendant at the end of the chain was going in a tight circle while Joan spoke in Old Gaelic.

She was communicating with the Fae and the spirits, asking for guidance. And they were responding.

The pendant went faster as it spoke to the spirits, each one feverishly searching for Bridget, doing Joan's bidding. None of this was visible to the eye but I understood the words if the rest didn't.

Finally, the pendant froze, and with it Joan. Declan glanced at me, ready for me to take the lead.

I approached the map, already suspecting the location since Dagda. But we couldn't take any chances. I had to be certain.

"Brú Na Bóinne, it's a portal to the Otherworld," I said, confirming Dagda's words.

"Otherworld?" Brian asked.

"Where the God's live," Joan whispered.

"Yes, Joan. It's where we live and the source of our magic. Brú Na Bóinne is one of many portals." I took a deep breath and began to tell them about my visit with Dagda.

And what it meant.

CHAPTER 5

The early morning was one of my favorite times of day. When the world was just waking up and the air was cool and filled with possibilities.

If it wasn't for Edward, I might be enjoying myself.

I was pretty used to it, though, so that was a positive if you think about it.

Searching the sky again I was sad I didn't see my friend. My raven would be lovely company on the trip. As it was I was alone, and for the first time quite lonely.

That's the way of things isn't it? I've been alone for years, and I haven't been lonely per se. I get a friend, albeit a bird, and suddenly I'm lonely without him.

Oh well, at least I was away from Edward. There's always a silver lining if you look for it.

And my first best man beneath me. I called him Seagull because I swore he could run so fast it was like he was flying. Edward said that was folly and named him Jim.

Edward lacked imagination.

I wasn't so lonely as long as I had Seagull here. He was a good horse, solid, unwavering. He listened, but he was not a pushover either. No, he could give as good as he got, so if you wanted him to do something he didn't want to, he'd make you pay somehow.

Usually, it was Edward suffering bites from "Jim," complaining that I somehow made the horse dislike him.

I think the horse knew as well as I did what an ass Edward was. So he treated him thusly.

And it only made me love my man more.

Yes, Seagull was a very silly name for a horse, but he was white like the bird, and he loved water. The horse went nuts when he could roll around in puddles after a good rain or if we found a pond or lake he was done for. A silly name for a silly horse.

I felt a little less lonely now, and I gave Seagull a pat for being such a good friend too. Choosing to focus on what I did have usually did the trick. If only briefly.

Sometimes briefly was good enough.

I started braiding the part of Seagull's mane that I could reach. He seemed to like it and I didn't need to show him how to get to town, he knew. And he didn't seem to be feisty today, so I trusted him to be good.

I was leaning forward halfway up his mane when I saw a raven. We were in town but not town proper just yet and I couldn't get myself to stop braiding when something black flew in my peripheral vision.

The excitement that I got from seeing the bird was only slightly alarming. I wasn't an excitable person.

But I missed the damn bird.

"Hey, little fella," I said as I gave him a wave.

There was an ear-splitting grin on my face that I was trying to subdue but I would be lying if I said I wasn't looking forward to seeing him all day. He comforted me somehow.

He cawed loudly and flew away, and I was a little sad he left so soon. But I was happy he said hello.

It's alright. It was time to get to business, anyway. I had to stop and get a potion for Edward's illness and see my father.

My father lived in town on his own and he and Edward did business occasionally. Edward had given me a bill he had written up for my father, and I was to receive the payment for it.

My father was first on the list since I passed his house first, and I only had a few hundred feet to go as it happened. I might have passed him if not for the raven.

Helpful bird.

I tied Seagull up near my fathers and found him at the front door. He was a stout man, built like a barrel, and I looked just like him.

Maybe less barrel-chested, but there was no questioning he was my father. Dark hair and dark eyes, the same long nose, but my skin was a shade paler than his, reminiscent of my mother. My mother had passed years ago before I was first married, and he never remarried.

"Thought I heard you," he said embracing me.

"I wasn't that loud, was I?"

"It's a parent thing. Come in."

My father had done fine for himself. His house was on the outskirts of town. It was in the Victorian style, moderately furnished with matching furniture. In truth, it hadn't changed much since the days my mother had furnished it, a small comfort.

He was a craftsman by trade, that's how he had known Edward. He used Edward for the wood for his projects. Arthur was a pleasant man that always smelled of sawdust and wood stain.

I loved my father. And so did he. He spent the next twenty minutes telling me this and showing me that before I even spoke a word.

"So how are you?" he finally asked as we took a seat at the kitchen table.

"Fine," I said.

He was already preoccupied again and started telling me about the next project he had lined up with the blacksmith. The two of them collaborated often, most of the smith's tools needing handles, he passed bigger projects onto my father.

This was all well and good and I enjoyed spending time with my father, but he had this quality of being overly charming when he wanted something. I was beginning to get a bad feeling about what he was going to say next.

"And so I won't have the money for Edward until at least a week or more. Just as soon as I get paid by Samuel," he said.

Samuel was the blacksmith and a good man. I'm certain my father was a good man. Terrible with money though.

I swallowed around the lump in my throat. Edward wasn't going to be happy. But I hadn't the heart to burden my father with that.

"That's alright. I'm sure Edward will understand," I said softly.

I'm sure Edward ought to understand, or maybe not. This wasn't the first time my father would owe him money. Frankly, I hardly understood myself. But what was there to do?

It was likely how I ended up married to the man, to pay off my father's debt. Not that my father would ever tell me.

If he had the money it was spent on something he wanted but didn't need. Sometimes he'd say it was essential to his work, and other times, it was a gift to himself because he worked so hard.

Neither of which was true. He was just a good bullshitter. He even fooled himself I think.

Or maybe he spent it on whatever lady friend he was rumored to be with that month. He never remarried after my mother but not for lack of trying.

"Here, take this to Edward for me, will you?" my father said as he handed me an envelope, sealed.

"Of course," I said graciously, though it was likely to only irritate Edward further.

A letter? Why would he send me a letter instead of the money he owes me? I could hear it already, Edwards's voice thunderous.

My father had gone on about high praises for me and Edward and how wonderful we were to him. How lucky he was to have us.

And so on and so forth.

I know he loved me. But he loved himself more.

We bid our farewells with empty promises of money and more visits and grandchildren. I was nearly to the apothecary before I came out of my daze.

Visits with my father tended to do that to me.

When my mother was alive, it wasn't so bad. For me that is. In reality, I believe my mother simply took the brunt of my father's insipidity. If that's what you could call it.

Like my husband's, my relationship with my father invariably left me wanting more. In particular, Thomas, all charm and no depth. Once you scratched the surface, that was it.

That wasn't fair. My father wasn't a cruel man, or mean-spirited. I suppose his only sin was selfishness. Maybe stupidity too.

The apothecary was quicker. I only needed something for his stomach. Some ginger ought to do the trick, and I grabbed a few other things to replenish our stores and Edward, too, I guess.

On the way out, I ran smack into Mary, dropping (and luckily not breaking) the medicine I had just acquired. She was a taller woman, slim, with lank blonde hair and piercing blue eyes. She was a servant of the Proctors and the same age as me.

Quickly stooping with mumbled apologies, she helped me pick up the items I had dropped. She was always pleasant to be around.

"Bridget! What are you doing in town?" she exclaimed once recognition lit her features.

"Oh, Edward has a touch of something. I was grabbing a few tinctures for him."

She responded, but I was distracted by a flutter of black feathers to my right. For just a moment I met the beady black eyes of my new friend, and curiously I felt fear. Shaking my head to focus again I turned back to her.

"I'm sorry, what was that?" I said as politely as possible.

"I said, what is it that Edward is ill with?" she said back sweetly.

But I saw her glance at the bird. My heart started beating faster. I really didn't want her to look at him for some reason.

"Just a stomachache, nothing too serious," I said back evenly.

Keeping my emotions in check had become an art form at this point, and I didn't see any suspicion in her eyes to signify that I had tipped her off. I really just wish I hadn't brought attention to the bird.

"Ginger, that's the best for a bad stomach," she said as she endearingly patted my hand.

Her maternal instincts always showed in her familiarity. A pat on the arm, a squeeze of the hand, all of those little reassurances you give children.

"Yes, thank you. I have some and a few other things to speed up his recovery," I said, smiling.

The bird flew off, and I was relieved, but I didn't look his way. Too afraid to bring more attention to him. Mary and I exchanged a few more pleasantries before I made my escape with excuses about the time of day and a long trip home.

We gave our best to the other families with promises of not being strangers. When in reality that's all we were.

Sure, we've met a bunch of times. Her boss was another of Edward's business clients. Usually, though, she could only say a few quick words before her duties called, and off she went.

I always envied her that, escape.

Again, lost in reverie, I ran into something else. If it were Mary, I would die of embarrassment. The new rumor would be that I was not all there.

I guess that was true, though, wasn't it?

Big hands swallowed my shoulders to steady me before I fell on my ass. Looking up into a strange man's face, I quickly made my apologies and thanks before I went to hurry on.

Even worse, the hand talkers would say I'm after husband number four. But, as Edward had said, there would be no more husbands for me.

My worst nightmare began playing out in real-time when the man wouldn't let go of me. I looked up at him then, all smiles, to ask him politely to let me go.

You catch more flies with honey than vinegar.

"Bridget," he said, and though I would have liked to know him, I didn't think that I did.

He was tall, and big, with dark eyes and dark hair the color of bronze in the sunlight. His handsome features made my heart skip a beat, and I was suffering a loss of breath. Either from the impact or *him*, I wasn't sure.

Looking at him, I had the weirdest feeling of deja vu.

But he looked so sad. I thought it was such a shame for a handsome man like him to be like he was now.

His mouth was moving, but I didn't hear a word he had said. He shook me a little, and the fear brought me to my senses.

"No, no, lass, I won't hurt you. I'm sorry I startled you. Are you all right?" he said soothingly like I was a skittish mare.

I nodded my assent. No, I was not all right, but why should I tell him anything?

Shit, he was talking again.

"I need you to wake up," he said.

I looked at him with a pained look. I'd not heard much or what he said, but what I did listen to him say didn't make a lick of sense. I focused on his accent; it was so strange and familiar in turns.

"Wake up?" I said, brows furrowed to express my confusion.

"Bridget, please, I don't have a ton of time here, and I think my window is closing more rapidly than I had hoped. I need you to remember me and wake up mo grá."

He said the last with such force that accentuated his accent, making his words guttural. But I think he just said, my love. His hands were still on my shoulder, and he was squeezing just a hair too tightly. And I found that I liked it. A lot.

I don't know why but I felt safe. Much like my new friend made me feel, the raven.

"Yes, Bridget, reach for that. Don't forget this feeling, please I beg of you. Just wake up; Declan needs you...*I* need you."

I didn't know who he was or who he was referring to, but I was planning on holding onto this feeling. It was delightful.

Out of the corner of my eye, I saw two hulking figures that snorted and shook, and I was immediately entranced. Oxen, if that's what you could call those monstrosities.

Beasts like those were something else.

They were huge, solid walls of muscle with horns so big they were almost comical. There was nothing funny about them, though. As they pawed the ground anxiously, I found myself sinking closer to the stranger. They were beautiful if frightening creatures.

"I thought they might help jog your memory. Well, Brigid's. That is Fea and Femen, they're your oxen. Or hers. It's confusing. I hope that you'll take them home with you, let them keep you company. Here."

He reached into my satchel where I had placed the items from my father and the apothecary. Pulling out the envelope from my father he waved it in front of my face.

"You won't need this now. Take them and tell your husband this is your father's payment. Your father won't care one bit if he doesn't have to pay, and Edward might like these two. At first at least. He won't like them if he hurts you again," he said as he gently grasped my chin in one of his large palms.

All the while he had spoken I sat in dumbfounded silence. He knew too much, was too familiar with me, touching me and rifling through my possessions.

"Who are you?" I said, not bothering to fight his touch.

The intimacy of the touch should have sent me into a panic, but I found myself leaning closer. Pressing for another centimeter of my skin to touch his for as long as he would let me.

To hell with the hand talkers.

"Ruad," he said.

The pregnant pause that followed felt like he was waiting for something to happen. Most likely my recognition but I had none. This magnificent stranger was still strange to me.

Though I would be lying if I didn't admit there was some silent alarm going off inside of me. Something I couldn't put my finger on.

But I wasn't sure if it was the indecency of being in an intimate exchange in public with a man who was not my husband. Or if it was something more.

He leaned in then and pressed a kiss to the corner of my lips. I should have pulled away. Maybe I would have pulled away. But I knew I needed to hold on to this feeling.

If not for this dashing visitor, then for myself. It had been so long since I felt much of anything.

"Take care, darling. I'll see you soon," he said in a whisper.

With one final heartbreaking look, he turned on his heel and was gone. I wasn't sure if I had spaced out again or not, but he was gone awful quick.

However, I was remarkably stunned.

I went to retrieve the beasts he had left with considerable trepidation when Mary called out for me. Biting my tongue, I turned to face her, plastering a smile on my face and praying I looked somewhat normal. The pain helped, so I bit harder.

"What are those!?" she exclaimed.

"Oxen," I said stupidly.

"Well, yes, but I've never seen any like those before. You didn't have them just before, did you?"

Shit.

"No, my father dropped them off just now. Payment for Edward," I lied.

"I thought you had said you saw your father before the apothecary?"

Did I? I scanned my memories of the conversation and came up blank. It's not impossible I said that.

"Oh, yes, but I couldn't bring them to the apothecary, you see, so he dropped them off just now," I said back. It was believable.

"And you'll just take them home all by your lonesome?"

That was the question.

"Oh no! My father will escort me."

"Well then, why did he bring them to town? Don't you pass his house on the way home?"

Why did she know where my father lived?

"Oh, he had some business to attend to, and it was quicker this way," I lied again smoothly.

"Where is he now?"

Why do you care?

"I forget, maybe the smith. You know how the two of them are. Thick as thieves." That part was genuine.

"They certainly are." She smiled at me.

Something about her demeanor was off. I couldn't put my finger on it, but I wanted to get away from her quickly. There was a touch of something in her eyes that wasn't usually there.

"Well, I must be on my way; it's pretty late already. It was lovely to see you again, Mary," I said as I began to shuffle my way to the giant animals.

I didn't get very far before I ran into something *else.* Reaching back I felt the fur first, so I chanced a glance back to see that both oxen had made their way to me.

Suddenly grateful I grabbed both of their reins and began a hasty exit. She just smiled at me and waved as I went, and I couldn't help but notice how nervous that smile was.

Was she always this weird, and I hadn't noticed?

What was happening?

CHAPTER 6

I had left the O'Connor's after my tale to go speak to Bridget. Walking in now, I was regretting not sending Joan and Brian home. These conversations were easier to have with Declan alone.

Trying to be quiet without alarming anyone I gently rapped on the door as I entered. No one answered.

Little bells went off in my head, but I was fairly certain nothing was amiss here. I'm sure it was just that I was on edge.

Going from room to room I peeked my head in before I finally found Declan in the library. He looked like a statue, and in fact, he was in very nearly the same position I had left him in.

Entranced by the fire, with one arm on the mantle, he didn't hear me until I rapped my knuckles on the doorframe. The noise didn't startle him, however, so he may have been aware of my presence, just ignoring me.

I felt guilty for intruding, but I wasn't about to leave.

"I was thinking about how to use this to our advantage, and I may have something," Declan said after a moment.

"How so?" I asked.

"If I could be cognizant maybe I could find her in there?"

"It would be a long shot. Never mind you would have to allow yourself to be taken by the queen. And if we pull this off, Bridget may end up killing us both for letting you do that."

"There isn't an alternative and we both know it."

I didn't answer, so he went on.

"What would give me the best chance, Ruad?" he prompted me.

"There is something. There are a few ingredients your mother may be able to get her hands on. She won't be happy to do it, though."

"She isn't happy now."

He wasn't wrong.

"You sent them home?"

"Yes, they need rest and I needed quiet. They mean well, but they drive me nuts."

I felt that way about Dagda, but I knew better than to say so. He heard everything. Probably even my private thoughts.

"Make me a list of the items, and I will send it to my mother," he said in a voice like gravel.

I took my cue to give him more air, and I went to the kitchen to write the ingredients down. It made me bristle every time I followed his lead, but I respected him too. Damn.

He met me in the kitchen minutes later. I'd grown bored by that time and began tea for the both of us. Lavender was in order by the state of affairs.

"And if I fail?" he asked me once he made himself comfortable leaning against a counter.

"She'll kill you." No use beating around the bush.

"And I spend eternity in the pits of hell?"

"As I understand it."

He nodded at that and was contemplative for a few moments.

"But you'll get her?"

"Eventually."

"In this lifetime?"

"I hope so," I said softly.

"She's been let down enough."

"She has."

He was quiet again for a while and I was beginning to wonder just what he was planning. I didn't anticipate being included in whatever he was hatching up.

I'm not sure that was a good thing.

"You'll let me know if you have something stupid up your sleeve?" I asked.

He gave me a quelling look, so I gave him a headache. Rubbing his temple idly, his look turned suspicious.

"Head hurt?" I asked as I handed him the tea. "This will help."

"Thanks," he said as he accepted the hot beverage gingerly, never breaking eye contact.

I might respect him, but it didn't mean I would take any shit. The headache would go away after the tea. A happy accident, the tea, but the message would remain.

I play nice because I am nice. But I wasn't a pushover.

Lugh could be arrogant too.

"A pissing contest won't help us any," he said softly.

"I didn't realize it was a contest," I quipped back.

He made to throw me against the counter, but I froze him in place. That was when I saw the first glimpse of fear in his eyes.

But it wasn't at me.

"She'll be alright, Declan," I said as I let him go.

He relaxed his muscles, but he was still tense. Rubbing the back of his neck he nodded in apology before turning his attention to his tea. Wrapping his hands around it, he brought it to his lips and took a giant inhale before a tentative sip.

Taking another, he then stalked off to the dining room to take a seat with me in his wake. Grabbing the seat opposite him, I waited until he spoke.

"How do you manage?" he asked finally.

I smiled at that one. Barely, I said in my head, but I said what would be helpful instead.

46

"Faith."

"In what?"

"The Universe, God, Odin, Dagda, whatever or whoever you want to call it."

"Easy for you to say."

He wasn't wrong.

"Your existence may end soon, to be sure. And what would you have accomplished? What happiness would you have had? You would die leaving no true legacy behind, no wife, no children, no one to sing your praises."

"Rub it in, Ruad."

"But your soul lives on, Declan. Your life span is not your soul's journey. Eventually, all will be well."

"But that doesn't mean I'll get to see her again."

"No, it doesn't. Maybe not this time around. Hopefully in another life."

"Hopefully for me, not for you."

I smiled in acknowledgment. If I had it my way, no, I wouldn't share. But when did I get that lucky?

"Was I with her before? In a past life?" he asked after a beat.

"Yes, more than once."

He was contemplative at that.

"So we're perpetual rivals?"

It was my turn to be pensive.

"I think it's more like two sides of the same coin. Light and dark."

"Opposites and yet the same."

"One can't exist without the other."

We were quiet again.

"You never asked how she was," I said finally.

It had been bothering me for quite some time now.

The smirk he gave me was gloating, if only a little. Reaching into his shirt he grabbed a chain and pulled until the charm at the end was revealed. Holding it up for me to examine he produced a silver series of knots, large for a necklace, and old.

"The Serch Bythol," I said knowingly.

"Aye, me mum had it," he said, the brogue thick with emotion.

An ancient symbol, the Serch Bythol was representative of everlasting love between two people, soul mates they'd say now. Composed of three Celtic knots known as triskeles, they were connected by two of the three knots, with the third on opposing sides. The triskeles represented each person's heart, mind, and soul, distinct and yet connected.

"You can tell how she is with that?" I was a little surprised at the emotion in my voice.

"Aye, something like that. I kept noticing I was sensing things I didn't usually. Well, things I haven't felt in years. Despair, agony, empty." He looked at me then.

I nodded, both in acknowledgment and to encourage him to continue. Those were the range of emotions Bridget was accustomed to lately.

"The emptiness was what got me. Got my mother too. I kept saying to myself I ought to be more upset, more worried, more *something.* Bridget is gone and in trouble and I just felt icy, cold, nothing.

"She took me aside to give me this before," he said, motioning at the necklace, "and I saw that look on her face. The one I always got when I was in trouble as a kid. Grief, that gaping hole of grief as a mother, wanting to help her child, and not knowing how.

"When I put the necklace on I felt all the other things. That ache in my bones, the weariness, that pit in my stomach. I don't think they were my feelings or not just mine.

"Because curiously enough, I thought that I heard you. I felt like you were here. Even looked around for you, called your name. But you were nowhere to be seen."

"You think that you heard me through Bridget?" I said a little baffled.

I'm all-knowing, but there's still that element of people that you can't account for. Just how much magic they have in them. How open they are to the Otherworld.

"I don't know what I think, Ruad. I may just be going crazy. But there's something *different* ever since I put on the necklace."

"So that's the inspiration behind your plan. You think you can connect with her like me with the necklace."

He shrugged.

"It's worth a try. She might wake up if it's me."

I rolled my eyes.

"Rub it in, Declan,"

He smirked. He had a point, and he knew it. She's met me in all of her lives. He would stick out.

Failinis stalked into the kitchen then, hackles raised. Glancing at Declan, I could tell he felt it too.

CHAPTER 7

Thwack, thwack, thwack.

Edward wasn't pleased, but ironically not about the two insanely large animals I had brought with me. Apparently, I had taken liberty with my freedom and arrived home much too late for his liking.

I wasn't aware I had a curfew, but I took my punishment in silence. It was over quicker that way.

Thwack.

I was also not allowed to look bored, so I got an extra one for that. Trying to look contrite, I stared at him from beneath my thick lashes until he was satisfied.

And when he turned his back, I rolled my eyes. I think he preferred that I cowered; maybe they all did. That's why I refused; my defiance was the only thing they couldn't take from me.

Feeling more like myself than I probably ever have, I tried to keep Edward from noticing. A giddiness followed me all the way home and was partially responsible for my tardiness.

I was busy relishing the sun on my face and the smell of an incoming storm on the summer breeze. I was listening to the drone of the cicadas in their ceaseless chatter.

It was late, as a matter of fact, but for once, I couldn't care less about what Edward had to say about it. There was a lightness to me that I refused to let Edward or anyone else snuff out.

I'm sure it had to do with the stranger in town. I'd have thought I was only hallucinating if Edward hadn't remarked about the two oxen that had followed me dutifully home. Even the last interaction with Mary felt like a dream, but she'd seen the animals too.

She had seen them and seemed oddly interested in them. I shuddered at the memory of her eyes at that moment, suddenly chilled to the bone despite the heat.

I went about heating up Edward a late dinner after he was through. He went out to accommodate our newest acquisitions.

The dunce had complete instructions on how to heat it, and yet he waited until I was home for me to do it. I'd told him to eat without me since I wasn't sure when I would be back. But of course, he didn't. I just wasn't sure if I should be appreciative or not.

Did he wait out of politeness or laziness?

The raven was back, cawing gently from his post on the little back porch. I nodded my hello, happy to have my friend back. There was something peculiar about him, though, and once I had a break, I went out to investigate.

He seemed agitated, and I was hesitant to get closer to him, afraid he had come down with an illness. I was slowly backing away when he unfurled his large inky wings and landed on my shoulder with urgency.

Peering at him with a nervous sideways glance I was able to see something in his beak. He nudged the side of my head with a wing and nodded his head, encouraging me to take it.

Grateful to look somewhere other than at his looming beak I opened my palm and held it up, wincing while I did so. My imagination had led me to believe it was a mouse or other small rodent—like cats do, presenting their owners with the fruits of their labor.

My stomach churned when a wet, warm, solid *thing* slithered into my hand. A slight shiver ran down my spine as I anticipated investigating my new gift.

Opening one eye, I saw the bird placing something else in my palm and was mildly relieved to see it didn't look furry. Once he removed his beak and sat back on my shoulder, I took a closer look at my bounty.

Two medium-sized dark stones sat where the bird had placed them. Both were smooth and glossy with one end rounded and the other pointed. They looked deliberate, like whoever had them previously had fashioned them to be tools. Like ancient daggers.

One was a brilliant red color like rust, streaked through with black dots of all shapes and sizes. The other was dark as night with a golden hue that shimmered when I moved my palm resembling my friend on my shoulder.

I was smiling despite myself—what a thoughtful little guy he was.

Moving my presents to my other palm, I used my now-free hand to pat his glossy feathers. He ruffled them a little and inched closer to my head to lean his body on mine briefly.

"This is the best surprise I've ever gotten; thank you, my friend," I whispered conspiratorially.

He bent his head down and peered curiously in my face with one beady eye. I think that meant you're welcome or something like it.

A dragonfly floated beyond his head in my peripheral vision. Peeking my head around his, I didn't see where it had gone, but it made me feel like I was forgetting something.

I gave him another pat, and he cawed gently back before flying to his perch. Turning to go back inside to continue preparing dinner, I froze when I saw Edward.

Just beyond the corner of the house, he was hidden in the shadows of twilight, casting light sideways through the trees. He made no move toward me any more than I made a move toward the house, but his stoicism was menacing.

I wasn't sure how long he had been there or what he had seen, but it was evident that he'd seen enough. Enough to be curious, at least.

The raven was back on my shoulder in a flash, and I was suddenly less nervous, for now. It was undoubtedly a show of support, for which I was immeasurably grateful.

But the bird wouldn't last as long as Edward's ire. I had to leave him, eventually. It wasn't as if I could have the bird with me wherever I went.

I didn't know what he could possibly be mad about. It seemed excessive that I not be allowed even a tiny, feathered friend.

I know he'd told me to shoo the thing away, but he couldn't really blame me if the bird found me again. But the set of his jaw and the squaring of his shoulders said all I needed to know.

Finally, he broke eye contact and went about his business, and I went about mine. I was fine for now.

Offering up my arm to my savior he hopped onto my proffered wrist where I was better able to give him a kiss. He just got better all the time.

"Would you like to come inside with me?" I asked him.

To hell with Edward. I'm taking him wherever he's willing to go with me.

He answered by flying to the door and waiting patiently beside it. Something buzzed in my brain at that, there really was something peculiar about this bird, but I was eminently grateful for it.

Letting us both inside, I took one more glance behind me, but Edward was nowhere in sight.

———

Dinner came and went uneventfully with Edward not speaking a word. He dutifully shoveled food in without so much as a glance in my direction.

I would have been terrified if I weren't so glad. A peaceful evening was a rarity, and I was savoring the calm. Plus, I was a little more than pleased to have my feathered friend as a dinner companion.

As I ate, I gave bites of food to the raven, alternating between myself and him. He waited his turn like any well-trained dog, never begging nor prodding me for more, trusting me to care for him. Similar to how I trusted him to have my back.

It was an intangible thing. An unspoken agreement between the two of us. We had each other's best interest in mind. And I appreciated it so much.

Once we had finished eating, Edward walked to the bedroom while I cleaned up. The raven and I cleaned up in companionable silence before heading to the bedroom together.

He hopped onto the open windowsill while I changed and settled in bed. Edward never moved. Neither did the bird.

CHAPTER 8

"She's too far gone, Declan. I don't know what to tell you," I repeated for the third time.

He was busy pacing and muttering expletives, but I wasn't surprised. She had to be open to the possibility of more. There had to be hope. Something she wasn't remotely in tune with.

"I thought the rocks would help," he said exasperated.

"They did. The obsidian will help protect her from attacks from the queen; they just didn't do what we wanted them to," I said again.

It was a chance worth taking but the significance was lost on her. She was shut off from the spiritual world, and I didn't think anything would make a difference.

"So the other plan it is," he said, at last, coming to stand in front of me in the wingback chair near the fire.

I was glad he was pissing me off with his ceaseless motion. It was a fruitless endeavor, and it made me want to throttle him.

Something in my countenance must have tipped him off to my black mood because he frowned suddenly. Scrunching up his eyebrows he gave me an inquisitive look I was reticent to answer.

"Come out with it already," he said after a beat.

I was secretly glad. It gave me a glimpse of the man I respected, not this blithering, hand-wringing idiot I'd been watching walk to and fro listlessly.

Raising my eyebrow at him he deflated a touch.

"Right, yes, I've got my faculties now. Now get on with it," he said with a thump as he sat in the chair opposite me.

"It's set in motion already. There's nothing to fuss about. You will willingly sacrifice yourself for her and we'll try to get you out. That's all there is to it."

He stared at me a moment before turning his attention to the fire. I studied it too, watching the long flames dance across the wood. Like dragonflies flitting about.

"What part bothers you most? That it's me making the sacrifice or that she'll mourn me if you fail?"

He was as sharp and blunt as his predecessor. Never skipped a beat.

"You're taking the risk. Doesn't sit right."

"Don't suppose it does."

Made me feel weak. I didn't like playing second fiddle.

"She didn't notice the engraving?"

"No, I thought she would have inspected it more, but she got distracted."

I was a little irritated then when she didn't notice the carving on the stones. The same symbol as Declan, the Serch Bythol, delicately set on each stone. It was a part of my black mood.

It wasn't like her to be so aloof. So unaware.

"It's inevitable," Declan said.

I inclined my head. We'd known it was, but it didn't make me feel any better about it.

"My mother nearly has all of the ingredients for the concoction," he announced at last.

Nodding my head again I let my gaze wander to Failinis sleeping in the corner. In his mistress's absence, it was as if he had become emotionally closer to her.

He slept now, as she did in the Otherworld. Just as he had alerted us to the danger, she was in.

Declan followed my line of sight and seemed to come to the same conclusion that I did.

"I ought to rest now," he said as he tipped an imaginary hat to me before making his way up the stairs.

I remained where I was, my mood worsening by the minute. Though Declan had been a nuisance to my frayed nerves, at least I wasn't lonely.

The quiet of the room felt suffocating and the damp evening outside did nothing to brighten the cloud surrounding me. I could take having her not be mine, but not having her at all made my bones ache with longing.

Everything felt hollow, and the emptiness threatened to swallow me whole. As if my stomach was twisted in knots of a black hole that was going to devour me.

"Quit your pity party," a voice said from behind me, Dagda.

A snap of electricity shot from me before I could stop it, the wild magic a manifestation of my stormy disposition.

"I've had enough of this pathetic moping. It has to be done; you know this," he spat.

Not bothering to look his way he continued to take the seat Declan had vacated. Stretching his long legs out in front of him, he leaned back, steepling his fingers on his stomach. It was such an arrogant pose, I thought, very assuming.

"And what of the Fomorians, Ruad? We've tried millions of scenarios; none are as suitable as this one."

"'Suitable,' what a word for your chronic abuse," I fumed.

To my surprise, he didn't take the bait. Still lounging, he merely raised an eyebrow at my attack.

"She's strong. You know that she's the only one capable."

"And you know there are alternatives."

"The scenario where you get to ride off into the sunset with my daughter and leave us exposed?"

"Exposed to what? The Fomorian's will self-destruct; they're disorganized, brutish, and stupid."

"We can't bet on that; it's too important. If we don't form an alliance, we risk losing the Otherworld to those brutes."

We'd been through this argument more times than I cared to recall. He sometimes mistook his being all-powerful for being all-knowing too.

"And when will she get a say?" I retorted.

He gave a derisive snort that sent another jolt flying wildly from me through the library. Specks of golden light could be seen in its wake, like my Bridget's magic.

"My daughter will do her duty," he thundered, though he made no motion. Only the steel in his eyes indicated his ire.

"Your daughter will wise up one day," I whispered.

"And? She is honorable and trustworthy; she would never forsake me for the choices I have to make for the betterment of our people."

"Aye, she is. Therefore she will abandon you for deceiving her into doing your bidding," I seethed.

"We'll see, won't we?" He shrugged.

And it was that, that arrogance that always did me in. His self-assuredness, particularly about his strong-willed progeny, would be his downfall. I couldn't wait to watch it happen.

"I trust you'll do the right thing, Ruad," he said at last before he was up and gone in a flash.

I turned the flames up higher with a flick of my wrist once he was gone. Adding another log to the inferno eased my need for destruction. If only temporarily.

Resisting the urge to burn the house down I made my way to the kitchen to put on tea. A habit of life with Bridget I grew to love tea, particularly the herbal remedies for my irascibility.

It was only Dagda that could bring that side of me to the forefront. But as my king and Bridget's father, I wasn't in a position to oppose him. Even my backtalk wasn't usually allowed, but he knew I was crucial to achieving his goals.

And that I had nothing to lose.

Returning after cheating by putting the mug in the microwave, I eased myself in front of the blaze once more and inhaled the lavender. No respectable Irishman was content with microwaved tea, but I needed the calming effects of the purple plant quickly. Beggars couldn't be choosers and all that.

Dagda may have constructed this from the start, this cycle. Set in motion long ago, before this Bridget existed. It made my blood boil more.

The Fomorians were forever trying to take the throne from Dagda. In every cycle, the Giants looked on the Druids with envy and malice, thinking their luck would surely change once they had the coveted title.

Brigid was crucial to ending this cycle in the mind of Dagda. Truly the strongest woman Ruad had the pleasure of knowing, she would need every ounce of her fortitude to marry a Giant.

And I would lend her every ounce of my strength if it killed me.

CHAPTER 9

I woke up feeling rested and delighted for the first time in a long time. Stretching luxuriously I saw my feathered friend on the sill, head tucked into his neck like a bitter wind was blowing.

There was no wind, nor cold, only the balm of a late summer morning that promised another hot day. Alerted by my groans of pleasure at gaining just the right angle for a proper stretch, my raven popped his head up to look accusingly at me.

"Sorry to disturb your slumber," I blurted before I realized my error.

Peeking guiltily at Edward, he didn't appear to be conscious yet. Sighing my relief, I winked at the bird to give him the "all clear," but he looked anything but relieved.

He looked worse for wear, and I threw the sheet off of me to inspect him closer. Joining him at the window he hopped onto the arm I offered him. I thought he was exceedingly careful not to hurt me as he settled with a few flaps of his wings.

His usual cheery temperament was a torrent of emotions I couldn't put my finger on, but it didn't feel good. It felt quite dismal in fact.

Smoothing the feathers back, I began to tiptoe my way to the other room where I wouldn't disturb Edward when the bird hopped off of me and onto Edward's shoulder. I started to shoo him vigorously, if quietly, when he gave a loud caw.

Wincing, I had my eyes closed for the impending maelstrom that Edward would rain down on me for inviting the bird in, but it never came. Peeking an eye open, the raven flew over to land on my shoulder, and I jumped out of my skin for a second, imagining him pecking my eyes out as I had wished on Edward.

He didn't, and I relaxed a little, but the feeling of dread was welling up inside of me. Worse than any abuse from my husband was the fear that he was my husband no more.

Inching my way closer to his still form I could see he wasn't breathing. I braved a touch to the skin on his neck, sitting on the bed and leaning over to do so, and found it icy.

All thought fled my mind as I sat there numb with panic. I couldn't move except to remove my hand from Edward and place it on the bed to brace myself.

The panic hit me like a ton of bricks, flooding my system with adrenaline and making me hyperventilate. When I tried to regain clarity, my stomach would twist again, and my vision got blurry.

What was I going to do? It was as if Edward had done this on purpose as one last lesson he would teach me. There would be no husband number four, he kept reminding me.

After a few debilitating moments of trying and failing to make sense of the situation, I got up to assess. Edward wasn't that long gone, I told myself to ease some of the discomfort. He couldn't have been!

It was still reasonably early, the first strands of sunlight straining through the trees before the sky was entirely blue. The suffocating breeze would be dew if it weren't so damn hot.

He had gone to bed before me, but I couldn't remember for the life of me if he'd been well then or not. Was he breathing when I came to bed? I would be asking that question for the rest of my life, I thought despairingly.

Checking him more, his stomach where he'd been curled on his side facing away from me was warm to the touch. But not warm enough.

"Shit!" I exclaimed, hands shaking uncontrollably.

My feathered friend exploded in a flurry of black feathers at my sudden outburst, and I felt guilty for alarming him. Ha! I felt guilty for scaring the bird, but I may have just killed my husband.

But no, I couldn't have! We ate the same dinner last night. The only difference was the medicine.

The medicine...

I blew past the man standing in the corner on my way to the medicine. Grabbing the open bottle I saw a dead dragonfly in the pool of sticky syrup that had dripped onto the counter.

Not puzzling in itself, the poor insect could have gotten stuck in the stuff. Or maybe he was on his last legs, anyway.

I guess the same could be said for Edward, he wasn't in his prime. That's all, it's just that he passed quietly in his sleep, as old men do. Old men in their fifties was a stretch, but I was at least content with that explanation.

Men...something was jumping for attention in my brain, but I wasn't picking it up. I was racking my brain when a noise came from the bedroom.

A man in my bedroom, that's what I couldn't remember. Even with that knowledge, it was like walking through water to get there.

My brain and my body felt like separate entities, each as slow as the other but not in tandem. As if the imaginary water had gotten in my head, drowning thought and depriving my limbs of the oxygen necessary to keep working.

By the time I made it to the bedroom there was a human shaped bundle of blankets on the floor I could only assume was Edward. The man was standing there with one hand in his dark hair and the other on his hip as he looked blankly at the lifeless shape on the floor.

I don't know if I walked quietly or not, the whoosh of blood pumping in my ears was deafening, but the man didn't move until I was in the doorway. In another part of my brain, I realized I should have been terrified, but I couldn't muster up the energy anyhow.

When he saw me my heart broke a little. The man from town. Tall and handsome and he kissed me. I wished he could do that now and make all of this disappear.

But there was no escaping this. Something in me knew it.

The look he was giving me reflected my own thoughts. Anguish colored his features, making his face flush red and dark eyes amber with emotion. The color was so familiar.

He didn't have any hope for me either.

I realized again that he must have been saying something by the way he started gesturing with his hands, but I hadn't heard a word he said. My mouth hung open like a fish out of water, and there was no moisture to be found.

Blinking a couple of times and trying and failing to swallow, the panic hit a fever pitch. Hyperventilating, my stomach lurched as adrenaline hit me like a ton of bricks.

And then I was panicking about how much I was panicking in front of a strange man, no less, and the tsunami of sensations sunk me to my knees. The man had followed my mental implosion because he had disappeared sometime before I collapsed.

Returning with water, wet cloth, and bread, he first placed the cloth on the back of my neck before situating himself behind me on the floor and cradling me to his front. Pulling my head back unceremoniously with a giant hand to my forehead, he leaned it against his shoulder, where he stroked my hair back from my temple soothingly.

Wrapping his other arm firmly around my waist, his hand came to rest on my ribcage. His hand stretched from hip to beneath my breasts with ease, branding me with his heat.

Muttering in a different language, he moved back until he could lean against the wall, pulling me with him. When he was comfortable, my breathing was almost even again, and I sank into him, suddenly exhausted.

"Análaigh," he said softly as he continued his rhythmic brushing of my hair.

The pounding of my heart was beginning to match his, beating strongly against my back. His deep voice was gravelly in my ear, and I could feel his breath blowing wisps of my hair with every incantation.

In the recesses of my mind, I knew I should be panicking more that he was here and holding me so intimately. But I would have given anything to snuff out the panic I had just been in.

And I would have given a great deal more to have this man hold me like this regularly. Well...maybe not quite like this.

Finally, almost level, I squelched the remnants of panic that welled up again before I collapsed entirely against him. Closing my eyes I breathed in the scent of him before I spoke. He smelled like the mountains. It was oddly familiar and infinitely comforting. Ruad, he had told me his name was Ruad.

"Thank you," I breathed at last.

Having no intentions of moving, I relaxed a little more into him. His answering chuckle told me he knew it was intentional but that he didn't mind. And I was eternally grateful.

"You're welcome, Bridget," he whispered as he kissed my temple.

I should argue, or move, tell him not to do things like that. But I would be lying.

"And thank you for that," I said after a beat, adamantly not looking at the object to which I was referencing.

He squeezed my ribs in answer, pulling me closer as he did so. Twirling locks of my hair around his fingers idly, he swept the rest of it to that side so he could run his fingers through the tresses, allowing the clammy skin of my neck the air it desperately needed.

"Who are you?" I whispered at last.

"Your Guardian Angel, I guess," he mumbled.

"Thank you," I said again.

"You can stop saying that now," he said with another squeeze.

"Well, I'm not sure what else to say."

"Don't I know it."

"How are you here?"

"Do you really not know?"

I thought about it for a beat. The trouble was I was so used to being wrong I was terrified to speak up.

Sensing my hesitancy, he tugged my hair, playfully encouraging me.

"The bird?" I queried.

"See? Not so scary."

"But you can't be a bird," I argued.

"Bridget, I need you to listen to me. You're under a spell and I need you to wake up."

"You keep saying that and I don't know what you mean! And you didn't answer my question."

"It was a statement, not a question. But there're a lot of things I can do as your Guardian Angel."

"Sounds more like the work of the Devil," I said.

I wasn't overly superstitious as far as that was concerned, but that was what they spoke about in church.

"Do you think I'm the work of the Devil or one of your late husbands?" he inquired softly.

He made a good point.

"The Devil is supposed to tempt us," I countered.

"I tempt you," he said teasingly.

It felt wrong to be teasing right now. To be so close to him. I grumbled in response and went to get up.

His arm was a vise, squeezing me against him once more. Only I didn't feel threatened or uncomfortable; it felt nice.

"Not yet, I have to wake you up. Tell me, does the name Declan ring any bells?"

I thought about it for a minute. And then some more. Something hummed in my brain, but I couldn't grasp it. Just a feeling of a thought. I shook my head no.

"Jane? Michael? Alice? Mary? Ann?" He said the list like each one was bound to make me remember something—a pause between each name.

I shook my head again, unease starting to creep in. How did I know he wasn't the Devil? Or even just a crazy man that had no business being here.

"Análaigh," he said softly, and I took a steadying breath.

His chest shook a little with silent laughter, and he shook his head.

"What?" I said a little sharply. I didn't see any reason to laugh right now.

"I keep speaking Gaelic and you understand me. Yet you don't remember anything. It's infuriating really."

"I don't know what you're trying to get me to remember and it's infuriating. Why would I speak Gaelic?"

"It's a little confusing. You are Bridget; you're in this life because the Queen of Elphame, who is a powerful fairy, kidnapped you. She's using you to get Declan.

"This isn't real, not in the way you think it is. Physically, you're in Ireland at a place called Brú na Bóinne, a portal to the Otherworld. We're trying to wake you up."

It sounded like absolute horse shit, but he seemed to believe it.

"Who is Declan?" I asked.

He did a deep sigh.

"He's your boyfriend, I guess. And he's a reincarnation of Lugh, a Celtic God, and king,"

"And what does the, oh..."

"Yes, the queen wants the king. But if she gets him, she will gain immense power in the Otherworld, and that's bad because she would try to overthrow Dagda, the ruler of that kingdom. And she's insane, so we really don't want a raving lunatic to rule the Otherworld,"

"And what does that have to do with me?"

"Well Declan would never willingly go to the queen, but he will if she has you."

"And she has me now?"

"Yes and we think we can get you out, but it would help a lot if you were awake. Awake, I could count on you to make your own way out and I could send you some assistance. Dreaming, I could possibly get you out myself, but I would be leaving Declan exposed and putting us all at risk. And if she still has you under her spell, she can use you against us."

I pondered that for a bit. As I thought, he brought the water then the bread to my lips, helping steady my shaky hands as I drank. My stomach protested, so achingly empty.

"Is that why you're so nonchalant about *that?*"

"Partially. Also, because I needed you to calm down and quickly, which humor does the trick for you."

"What do you know about me?"

"A lot. Like how you can't be too upset about *that.*"

Not wholly.

"And how am I supposed to wake up?"

He was quiet then.

"Well, we think just awaking your subconscious should help, so I keep trying different ways to ring your bell, but they don't seem to be working."

"I wonder why not," I said.

"You have to have faith in more. This life you've lived never gave you a chance."

"A chance at what?" I snorted.

"Exactly."

"So why bother then? Why bother trying to wake me if you know you can't?"

"Tell me, are you happy?"

"No,"

"I mean right now,"

He got me.

"Yes," I whispered.

"I give you what comfort I can, mo grá."

"Thank you."

We were quiet for a while. The silence stretched as the morning sun made its way into the sky and woke up the rest of the wildlife.

"What do I do?" I asked finally.

"Not much to do darling, the queen will be here shortly."

"Why?"

"She has to control you, so she will be here to put you further under her spell."

"You can't stop her?"

"Not here. This is her realm; she's too powerful,"

"What is she going to do to me?"

"Do you really want to know?"

A sharp series of knocks sounded at the door, and I bolted upright in his arms. My heart tripled in tempo a second after.

"It'll be alright, mo grá," he whispered.

"You said I had a boyfriend, but you keep calling me your love. Why?"

"Can't I love you too?"

I supposed so.

68

As we both got up, he kissed my forehead once before transforming into the raven once more. It gave me comfort that he wasn't leaving me just yet.

CHAPTER 10

I flew up to the rafters to keep watch, and I saw Bridget find me once more before opening the door. Steeling herself, she straightened her back, put her shoulders back, and took one last breath.

"Mary! How can I help you this morning?" she said.

I winced a little, feeling the magic pulsing off of this Mary. My only hope was that I went unnoticed since her hostility was mainly directed at Bridget.

Unfortunate, but fighting the queen right now wasn't part of the plan. As long as I didn't have to do any magic myself, I shouldn't be too noticeable.

In her madness, the queen leaked energy like a sieve; it was astounding that Bridget hadn't noticed it earlier. If she did, she discounted it, not trusting her intuition in this life.

The queen, known to Bridget as Mary, mumbled something I couldn't hear, and Bridget opened the door wider.

"It's not a good time right now, Mary." Bridget sounded thin, her borrowed strength zapping quickly.

"Oh, I'm sorry to be a bother, I just came to see if you were all right. You seemed out of sorts yesterday," she lied smoothly as she slithered her way past Bridget.

I could see movement beyond Bridget, shadows in the window next to the door. The cavalry was here already.

"Well, thank you, I'm sorry to alarm you, but everything is fine."

Shit, maybe I should have told her.

The waves of euphoria that roiled from the queen made the room smell like her magic. It was a heady mix of floral notes and sulfur and wild.

Her questionable choices were to thank for the sulfur that tainted her magic. Making deals with the Underworld leaves its mark.

Bridget's earlier comment about my being the Devil came to mind, and I worried for her. Being so disconnected from the spirits, herself, and reality, left her extremely vulnerable.

I was glad that this was only in her head. Though her experience of it was authentic, the reality in which this happened long ago was much ghastlier.

That time around, transforming from a bird to a human would not have flown, so to speak. Or maybe it would have if I had tried. But there was no use for regrets right now.

In contemplation, maybe she's not so far gone. I was able to show her my proper form, and she took it in stride.

Alarmingly well, actually, so my estimation that she wasn't so far gone may indeed be very wrong. She might be extremely disconnected from reality, delusional even.

"Oh, I'm glad to hear it! How is Edward?" the queen asked.

I felt Bridget's fear spike from here, and my heart broke for her. But now she had her confirmation.

Mary had killed Edward, switching out the medicine with poison. Or perhaps having had the apothecary mix a fatal brew before selling it to Bridget.

The queen looked like the cat that got in the cream, her mouth stretched in a wicked grin. But my Bridget held her ground, though I knew what it cost her to do so.

"Edwards unwell," she said simply.

"Right, yes, the medicine you had bought yesterday. Has it made him feel better?" the queen prodded.

"Yes," she responded.

I could feel the anger boiling from the queen, but she was trying to pace herself. Bridget had not uttered a lie yet—

untruths sure. But Edward was unwell, though he felt nothing anymore.

This wasn't the response that the queen had anticipated. Likely she had thought to find Bridget a nervous wreck, much like she was before. As she had been when these atrocities happened in the past.

If Bridget could stave her off for a while we may have a fighting chance. Mainly when Declan was able to get here.

The queen knew she was out of strict niceties and ought to take her leave, but she was battling the satisfaction she was anticipating. Teetering between calling Bridget out or re-strategizing.

The pull was too strong. That high she got from destroying her enemies was addictive, and it won.

"I had some business for Edward; might I speak to him before I leave?" the queen tried.

"Edward won't be doing business anymore, Mary. But you already knew that didn't you?"

That's my girl. She might be spiritually out of alignment, but she wasn't dumb. She knew she was playing with fire, but she would do it with her head held high.

The queen visibly bristled, haughtiness taking over her features. She tried for a wounded look after the initial slip and only mildly succeeded.

But it was too late.

"Why would I know that? What's happened to Edward?" Her voice lifted with the intonations of innocence.

"Because you killed him, Mary. That was the reason for the look yesterday, and that's why you're here now. The dead dragonfly in the medicine. What poison did you use?"

"You killed him, sacrificing him to the Devil to practice witchcraft. That's what they think, at least." She nodded her head towards the door, giving up the charade.

72

No one would believe Bridget over Mary, and the queen knew it. So did Bridget, but she wouldn't give up without a fight.

"As I sacrificed Samuel and Thomas? How? Making Thomas an idiot and Samuel miserable?"

"Witchcraft is poorly understood, Bridget; it's the fear that matters."

At that, the queen exclaimed loudly enough for her counterparts to hear and come to her aid. As they came rushing in to rescue her, she swooned.

There was no other word for her overdramatic rendition of a woman fainting, but the poor saps that came in were none the wiser. The concern that etched their features for "poor" Mary turned to ones of disdain and contempt as they looked at Bridget.

Bridget didn't stand a chance. Fists clenched in outrage at her unfair treatment looked awfully condemning if you thought she was a witch, out to get Mary. And Mary's prone body lying limp near her, as if she had fainted.

There wasn't a jury that wouldn't convict Bridget now, with so many witnesses. Anything Bridget said wouldn't matter either; it would be looked over as a desperate attempt to avoid the gallows.

But to the gallows, she would go.

The uproar took Bridget by surprise and her anger was truly something to behold. As the men who accompanied the queen attempted to place Bridget in shackles, she kicked and screamed and lashed out at them.

She tried to shock the acting Mary into awareness with shouts and curses but to no avail. I knew Bridget knew her actions only ensured her damnation, but she was past caring.

Hurling all of her pain and anger at the queen only served as some respite from all of the misery Bridget had endured. But at least the queen deserved it.

And Bridget had nothing left to lose.

As she screamed, I flapped my wings until I caught her attention before flying out of the window. I wanted to be sure she knew I wasn't abandoning her but there was nothing left I could do for her right now.

I watched from the roof as they dragged her away, the fight going out of her as the object of her ire was no longer in view. The men holding her captive were doing a job, and she had enough clarity to understand that even if they hated her.

Cawing loudly before she was placed in the carriage I saw the faintest smile on her lips before she was incarcerated. It gave me hope.

————

Back with Declan, I briefed him on the events of Bridget's arrest and the death of her husband, glossing over specific details.

"She's alright though?" he inquired.

"Better than she was; nothing pissing her off couldn't fix."

"That bad?" He chuckled.

"You've never seen her angry?"

"Little cause to. Agitated, sure, but never beyond control. Felt it, though," he said as he grabbed the symbol around his neck.

"Well, it may be your lucky day because you're up next."

"Aye, that I am."

The plan was for him to attend the trial. The public unrest was extraordinary, and he would be one voice among many. He also had creative liberty because the queen wouldn't be anticipating him, nor could she do anything to him with the spells I had placed on him.

The trouble was that we weren't at all sure he would be able to do anything. He might only have a loose handle on himself in there, and even if he were in complete control, Bridget might not wake up, anyway.

In my absence, Declan had called his parents to the house and sent his siblings out of town. This way, we would be able to protect his parents. His siblings were most likely out of the crosshairs but sending them out of town would decrease the chances that they found themselves in them.

Joan was currently in the kitchen preparing the concoction with Loretta. Meanwhile, Tommy and Brian followed Joan's instructions on placing protection spells around the house.

If the queen discovered Declan's intentions, she would attempt to sabotage him, so we were trying to be prepared. She wasn't likely to attack him herself, not with me around, but she had plenty of henchmen she could send.

And if her henchmen failed, as Carman had, she had spells powerful enough to harm. Even if she was doing them from a distance like Brú na Bóinne.

So we prepared the best we could. I'd summoned Senan, the clurichaun, to aid Declan in his dream state.

The little man's magic was suited for the task. Weaving in and out of worlds without detection was his forte.

Joan entered the room carrying a steaming mug. For perhaps the first time that I'd seen her, she looked nervous.

"It's ready," she declared.

Declan took the mug cautiously and set it on the end table near the couch he had chosen to doze on. He'd insisted on the sofa, stating that he thought he would have better control if he didn't sleep too soundly.

Embracing his mother in an engulfing hug, he patted her gently on the shoulder before letting her go.

"I'll be fine," he ensured her.

“Just get her home,” she said softly.

“Aye,” he said and downed the hot liquid in three large gulps.

Lying down then, he was asleep almost instantly.

CHAPTER 12

The jail, as it were, was a building in the town center with dungeons that were windowless and made of stone. Escape was hardly an option unless I were indeed a witch.

Having no windows meant no light and no air. The staleness of it was musty and made me sneeze.

There was no bed, only hay and a chamber pot to fill the space. I hardly needed use of either because I couldn't sleep for the hunger, and the water they rationed me was insufficient.

So I sat and bode my time while they decided what they would do with me. Occasionally one of the more brutish men would interrogate me to admit my wrongdoing and beat me when I didn't confess.

But I had nothing to confess to. And abuse was a part of daily life, hardly a deterrent.

It only made me more resolute. I wasn't stubborn; I was persistent, as my mother used to say.

And I would persist in my innocence long after the breath had left my lungs. Hell hath no fury as a woman scorned.

The sound of rattling chains came from the door before it swung open. A chair with chains attached to it was being carted into the room by the large man that tended to my punishment.

I didn't suppose it was there for my leisure.

The panic ratcheted up at this fresh hell they had planned for me. But I knew I wouldn't break. It just would fucking suck.

I sat silently while they situated the new torture device. When they grabbed me to seat me in it, I didn't argue or resist. Even though they didn't need to be so rough about it.

When they had me chained hands and feet to the chair, I bit my tongue to abate the surging terror. But they all left the room.

Extremely confused but entirely content for now, I relaxed a little into the contraption. It was not meant for comfort, but in all honesty, it beat the straw and the packed dirt that served as the floor.

I was not left to lounge for long, though. When the door swung open after maybe a quarter of an hour, I was surprised to see Mary waltz in.

And waltz she did, the pep in her step in stark contrast to the surroundings. She even finished with a twirl, skirts cascading in a large circle, engulfing the small space highly inappropriately.

"Oh, you look miserable!" She squealed in delight, the madness dancing in her eyes like the flicker of candlelight.

She came closer to examine my face. I adopted as bland a look as I could imagine, but I felt the fire in my eyes.

If looks could kill.

"Now don't be like that," she admonished, "this is for the good of the kingdom. You should be thanking me.

"Your sacrifice will do wonders for the Otherworld. They've been looking for new leadership for a long time, and you're going to help me do that."

"What are you talking about?"

"Oh!" she tittered. "Right! I forgot you have no memory! Let's see if we can't fix that."

She waved her hand once over me, muttering in a foreign tongue. It sounded like the same language Ruad spoke to me in, but she said it so low I couldn't discern the words.

A flood of images flashed in my mind, leaving me gasping for air. The sudden influx was confusing and overwhelming.

78

Ruad, a familiar-looking Goldman, creatures of every size and shape, an impossibly massive city, and green eyes.

Green eyes flickered by, but I pulled them back to me, focusing on them. All I saw were green eyes and freckles, but they soothed me.

My eyes were unfocused when she started speaking again, but I mainly had my faculties again. More so than I wanted her to know.

"So you understand me now! Now you know, I need this to work.

"Once I've secured Lugh, no one can stop me from taking the throne. Dagda and his ilk can find a place to rot." She spat at that.

"The Otherworld is sick of his rule. Me most of all. And once I've taken my rightful place as queen, I'll send your precious Declan to hell so I can rule unencumbered.

"Then I can deal with Ruad. Pesky bugger he is, he knows nothing, you know?"

She looked at me then, and I did my best deer in headlights look. It wasn't difficult to achieve.

"And you! I'll get to keep torturing you! Brigid, so wise, and yet so stupid! You didn't even recognize me when I was that wretched maid.

"Ugh! Possessing her gave me a headache; she was so *good* it made me want to puke."

I was slowly putting the puzzle together in my head. Why was it that villains always gave you their master plan? Just a habit of pompous bastards to want to brag about their genius all the time.

"Well, I don't want to ruin *all* of the surprises I have planned for you. There must be some excitement after all!"

And at that, she came and kissed me full on the mouth. The urge to bite her stupid face came to mind, but I resisted. If I didn't make her too mad, I might be able to use this.

In a whoosh of skirts and a wink, she floated out of the room, closing the heavy door behind her. I did some deep breathing to clear the cobwebs, but it seemed like she'd left my memories intact.

My real memories, that is.

Brain racing through an assortment of disjointed memories, I felt like I had been drugged. And maybe I had been.

A spell maybe, that might be more like it. Closing my eyes tightly I was trying to remember what my last real memory was.

It was like trying to remember where you left your car keys. You seem to remember them everywhere but the last place you had them.

She mentioned a maid, but I don't remember a maid. I certainly didn't have a maid. Nine hundred square feet didn't require a cleaning service.

No, not my apartment, Declan's. My brain lit up at the mention of his name.

Declan.

My friend, but not quite anymore. We went to his house; I was in danger.

But it was the queen, or Mary, who wanted Declan. Right, to stage a coup in the Otherworld.

I could feel I was almost there, but it wasn't quite right. There wasn't a maid at his house, was there?

Digging deeper for the sequence of events I felt like I only got more confused. Time was evading me, and I wasn't sure if what I remembered was yesterday or weeks ago.

That was when the door swung open again. All thought evaporated when I saw all manner of torture implements being carried into the room.

It was the same man, and he looked nearly gleeful when he saw the sheer terror in my face.

What was I being tortured for again?

Somehow, I don't think the queen gave me back my memories because both realities were very dreamlike right now. Like a fog had descended in my brain, muffling everything.

Well, everything but what I was experiencing. This was more like a nightmare.

———

I awoke sometime later, my mouth dry and metallic tasting. Licking my lips, I winced immediately. The bottom one was cracked and bleeding still and very swollen.

The good part was that eventually my body had enough of the abuse, and I passed out. That seemed to be what ended my battery this time.

Slowly coming to, I remembered the worst of the torture, and I glanced at my hands—five missing fingernails, three from the left hand and two from the other.

I was also missing my wedding band. Not that I cared that much about the thing, but it was mine after all.

My stomach churned, and I dry heaved, but there wasn't anything in it to throw up. I was glad at that, still tied to the chair in a windowless room. If I'd thrown up in my lap, I would never stop for the stench.

It took a long time to make up from down as my head spun. Keeping my eyes shut against the maelstrom, I was curious about what was causing it.

Dehydration, fatigue, hunger, or a concussion. Hell, maybe all four.

Practicing deep breathing, I tried to focus on other things. Familiar green eyes stared urgently at me, and I had to open mine to be sure that he wasn't there.

The brown ceiling met my gaze before the world tilted on its axis, and I had to shut my eyes again. My stomach was doing horrible flipping and flopping, and I was panting to cool my clammy skin.

He was not there, and I would not do that again anytime soon. The blood was rushing in my ears louder than a waterfall, and I waited until that abated before trying to think again

Everything felt far away like I was underwater. Even after the deafening whoosh subsided, it was hard to decipher noises.

I knew I was in the jail basement; the cold earth gave a permanent chill to the stagnant air. Any sounds I could hear were muffled, but I was fairly sure what I heard was animal sounds. That led me to believe it was late in the night.

A lack of any window meant my feathered friend couldn't visit. If I could even call him that now.

I wondered if he was able to become a rat. Then he could come to visit me in here.

Not that I could open my eyes to see him. But at least I wouldn't feel so alone.

Or maybe I still would. Rats wouldn't improve the surroundings, especially ones I could hear but couldn't see.

Trying to think straight, I took a deep breath, and a familiar woodsy odor hit my nostrils. Not trusting my eyes, I spoke aloud but heard nothing in response.

Following the train of thought brought up by the smell I thought of woods. Not just the smell but the deep twilight that cascades light through the leaves.

I felt as if I were surrounded by them, the trees talking with me like old friends. It was a calming place, one I vaguely remembered.

82

My battered hands relaxed against my skirts as I leaned into the feeling. Something hard met my left hand, and I struggled to recall what was there.

Lifting my hips, I was able to get my hand near the pocket there but not close enough. I was going to have to look to see how close I was, but I was reticent to try just yet.

Recalling the bird giving me the stones made me think of Ruad. I thought the black of the stone matched the color of his hair and his eyes. Dark with golden highlights.

The other stone I recall being a reddish color, freckled with black. Those haunting green eyes with their surrounding freckles came into view, and I got the impression that red hair would top the face I was pulling into consciousness.

The exact shade was troublesome. Not quite red, nor really blonde, the copperish color was near the color of rust but much more brilliant. Once the hair was there, the complete picture was easy to place.

Full lips and a vibrant smile pulled up in mischief made the green eyes dance, and I smiled despite myself. So that was Declan.

I wasn't sure who he was to me, but I was happy to see his face. Having a clear picture of him in mind, I let the rest fade away as I slipped back into a fitful sleep.

———

I don't know how long I was down there, but it felt like days had passed, and yet no time at all. I was abruptly woken up by the heavy door flying open. My assigned torturer was in company, but a small man led the party of people in a suit.

He was pointing at me and muttering, but I was nowhere near aware enough to follow what was happening. The chains that held me were released, and I was half carried out of the room.

I was eventually settled in a room, also devoid of windows but infinitely airier. If I had to guess, I was in the courthouse, hopefully awaiting a lawyer.

When my eyes grew too heavy to continue to analyze the room's features, I laid my head on the table to doze. I'm not sure how long I was out, but when I awoke, there was a glass of water on the table.

Desperately gulping the cool liquid down, I used what dribbled from my chin to clean my face with a handkerchief I had hastily. Blinking away sleep I noticed movement from the corner, and I nearly screamed from fright.

The bright smell of leaves met my nose, and I settled down.

"Do you live in the woods?" I asked him.

His warm chuckle was a balm to my frayed nerves. Waving one hand I saw the water glass refill itself.

"Thank you," I murmured, taking a few gentle sips. Gulping it as I had was not sitting famously in my very empty stomach, but I was still parched.

"Are you hungry?" Ruad asked, coming closer to the table.

"I couldn't eat if I was," I replied honestly.

"I thought so."

He smiled wanly and took the chair opposite me. Stretching out his long legs, he crossed his arms over his chest and gave me a once over.

I didn't pull my hand back quickly enough.

Grabbing hold of my battered hand gingerly, he placed a kiss to my knuckles, avoiding my fingertips. Muttering softly to my hand I felt the pain ease instantly.

"Better?" he queried.

"Much." I squelched the urge to thank him again.

I owed him more than words.

The headache and hunger pains left next, and I slumped in appreciation. Even the fear that gnawed at my insides eased in its intensity.

He seemed satisfied at my apparent comfort and settled more himself. Only my impending demise stood in the way.

"Are you okay?" he asked at last.

"Sure."

And I was I guess. At least I wasn't alone as I had been for so long. It was a comfort to have a companion.

"What do you remember?"

"Not much. More than I did, but it's like smoke. I grab onto something, and it floats away.

"I remember Declan's face, but I don't exactly know who he is or why he is important. And I know Mary is a witch, but I'm the one that is being tried for witchcraft."

He frowned at that but said nothing, so I continued.

"She mentioned he would help her rule the Otherworld."

"Did she? What else did she say to you?"

"Not much. She mentioned a Lugh and a Dagda, but I don't know who either is. And that she would continue to torture me, but I was pretty sure I was not going to be around much longer, to put it politely."

"Well, that largely depends on you, but it doesn't seem as if you've been able to break the spell."

I shrugged, unsure of how to break it.

"Lugh is Declan, or a reincarnation of him. Dagda is the ruler of the Otherworld that she wants to overthrow. And she will continue to torture you in your next life unless you can shake her hold now."

"Well, how do I do that?"

"I thought you'd wake up once you started recalling your other life, but since that hasn't happened, maybe you still lack faith, or the queen has different magic at work," he said matter-of-factly, but he came across concerned.

"What kind of magic?"

"I'd been thinking it was a simple sleeping spell, keeping you in a dreamlike state. But your confusion might mean she's delved into blacker magic."

"Like what?"

"Like a hex bag. What do you know about magic?"

"Black is bad."

"And?"

I pondered that for a while. What did I know?

In retrospect, I ought not to have known anything about it. It wasn't merely taboo in town. It was the work of the Devil.

By all means, my understanding of magic should be that it's all bad. And yet, I knew there was a difference.

It was evident in the trust I had for my feathered friend turned *supernatural handsome human* friend. When he filled my water, I drank without hesitation.

I'd spent quite a bit of time in his arms during my panic attack, and I felt comforted instead of nervous. *And I had let him kiss me.*

I didn't *know* anything per se. I *felt* enough though.

"I can feel the difference," I said at last.

He smiled, a genuine one that made butterflies erupt in my belly. It seemed as if I had passed some test.

"It's a start," he acknowledged.

"A start of what?"

"I wasn't sure you were even this aware of what was going on, but following your intuition is a good sign that you at least trust yourself, if not me yet."

Didn't I trust him? I felt the resistance like a punch in the gut.

"Not as much as I need you to."

86

"Why? What would I need to trust you more with?"

"Do you know what is in store for you? Outside of this room?"

The fear twisted my stomach in knots at the mention. I nodded affirmatively not wishing to speak.

"It's not ideal. But I think it may help reset your memory enough to break the spell. Black magic feeds off of suffering, and you've had plenty of that, but what comes next is worse.

"The queen will get stronger from more of your suffering, but so will you. Just promise me you will hold on to that feeling, the hope."

I nodded, and he got up, rounding the table to my side. Kissing the top of my head one second he was gone the next.

CHAPTER 13

I left Bridget in search of Declan. On this side, he needed all the help we could give him.

I found him wandering around outside the courthouse. He didn't seem all that lucid.

Senan was walking beside him, using his magic to appear human. When I queried Senan with a look, he merely shrugged.

Stepping in front of Declan to stop his progress, he looked at me confused before walking around me. It didn't appear that the tea had the effect he had hoped it would.

I looked at Senan for help, and he waved his hand in a wave of magic at Declan that stopped his progress but did nothing for his state of mind.

Great.

I nodded my head in the direction of the courthouse and Senan caught my drift. If we could get him in the door and into a seat that might be enough.

With another wave, Senan steered sleepwalking Declan in the right direction. In all sincerity, I had doubted this plan would bear any fruit, but there was the chance Lugh's magic may be more potent than I'd like to admit.

Declan seated, I dismissed Senan to look after his family. I took the seat next to Declan and performed an animation spell around us. This way, we could sit silent and motionless like Declan was, and I preferred to, without seeming odd.

Though it was a dreamscape, it was advanced because people did interact with us. And we could influence them.

For that, I would need to pay attention to what was going on so we could appear to react appropriately. Which wasn't difficult because I did need to be alert for the queen.

I didn't get the sense that she was aware of either of us here but just in case. When she was aware of us she wasn't going to be pleased.

The entire town was in attendance. Bridget's hell was a matter of public gossip and judgment.

Chaos was the reigning feeling in the room. People sat, stood, fidgeted, whispered, and shouted at random intervals while more streamed in.

There was no order yet, no judge to enforce it. The public outcry over witchcraft was a heady mix of fear, loathing, and a little reverence borne out of self-preservation.

No single person wanted to face the witch, but together, they felt strong in their numbers. The afflicted Mary was subject to fits of twitching and random outbursts.

That was what brought Bridget to court and would bring many other men and women to trial for witchcraft during this time.

The Salem Witch Trials would prove to be a monumental period for various reasons. There was no innocent until proven guilty yet, and the accused were denied lawyers.

It was the guilty proven guilty, except they're not. Innocent lives were put to the stake for absurd reasons.

It's jealous wives who point their fingers at the maid, maybe because she doesn't like how her husband looks at her. And neighbors call out neighbors because they don't like the way they dress, or talk, or maintain their property.

Where the real guilty ones just manage to point the finger first.

This atrocity would be studied for years to follow. The psychology of crowds, the science of society, the measure of what constitutes justice.

What happens here isn't justice; it's hypocrisy. A bunch of good God-fearing people assigning others to death.

Love thy neighbor is what they say aloud, yet they condemn them all the same.

And Bridget is first at bat. How lucky for her.

The judge presents himself at last, Judge Hathorn. This is only the first day of many that Bridget will be put on display like a sideshow freak.

It's asinine, the idea that the accused is going to admit their wrongdoing in a fit of clarity suddenly. If you ripped out my fingernails, I would tell you what you wanted to hear.

The punishment for not telling you is more torture. And the punishment for telling you is death.

It hardly makes a difference, but I'd sooner accept death.

But then again, I knew the outcome here. If it were me and I didn't know I would probably be put to death with no limbs left.

As would Bridget if she thought she had a fighting chance. Though they don't let it go that far, not yet.

Later in the trials, the torture gets more inventive and less humane. Bloodthirsty only begins to explain it.

In the scope of human history, it's a step up. Being drawn and quartered was among the worst ways to go. The guillotine might be the way to do it if I had to, as long as the blade was recently sharpened.

Order brought to the court lasted only a moment before murmurs began anew. Occasionally some brave souls shout their disapproval again.

Judge Hathorn bangs the gavel and menaces disapprovingly, but he's visibly as influenced by the excitement as the crowd. As if there was a wave of energy radiating off of his body, reverberating with that of the masses.

Once silence descends again, he begins his spiel, recounting the many claims against Bridget. Five women accused her of bewitching them, causing them to twitch and have outbursts.

90

That they saw her spirit in their bedrooms, pulling them from their slumber.

Naturally it's all hogwash.

Most condemning is the deaths of her husbands. As the saying goes, fool me once. This is thrice for Bridget.

At the culmination of Judge Hathorn's recitation, he calls on the first accuser, Abigail. A girl really, she wasn't yet a teenager, and her slim figure seemed swallowed up by the seat.

As we sat and listened to her account of Bridget's figure whispering to her asking her to commit heinous crimes, I was appalled at the nature of the accusations. From the mouths of babes.

Declan was still motionless beside me, though even without any magic, I'm certain no one would have noticed. Abigail had a captive audience for her claims.

Whether it was, in fact, the queen, the girl's imagination, or something else entirely, I didn't know. Bridget wasn't the first to be tried for witchcraft in the reality the queen had recreated, nor was she the last.

Many were tried, plenty acquitted, still others that had lost their lives during the frenzy. Bridget was just another face in the crowd.

Truth be told Bridget *could* be responsible for the apparition the girls claim to have seen. An unexpected consequence of her deprivation from the spirit world from which she hailed.

Magic unused doesn't dry up and disappear. Much like the law of motion, for every action is an equal and opposite reaction. It can't be destroyed. It simply changes.

Bridget's magic is like a tea kettle; the water warmed to the boiling point must be used for good, or else it became steam. It was burning the kettle in its haste to escape, to be helpful.

But I'm confident that Bridget's spirit would be good and kind. That it would be helpful.

Perhaps it's merely a combination of the above. Mass hysteria, underutilized magic, and pettiness. For the queen, an opportunity.

I had seen this scene before, though, so I examined what I maybe wasn't focused on the first time around. Like the way Abigail glanced surreptitiously at Mary as she spoke.

It was a similar manner to the way Judge Hathorn did.

Mary, however, was staring at me with daggers in her eyes. The illusion I was using masked Declan's immobility and our identities, not the magic used.

She couldn't break the spell, but she could sense it. I was stronger than her by far, smarter, more powerful. I could disband the magic she'd used against me and strike her down where she sat with a snap.

The trouble was her band of merry men. She was insane, flawed, not nearly as strong as even her followers. Yet, they followed her all the same.

The devil you know is better than the one you don't.

The queen was predictable only in her madness. She was capricious, petty, jealous. But I could count on it.

If we went after her now, there was no guarantee what her posse might do. That was where the danger lay.

Even psychopaths had friends. Dangerous ones at that.

I thought back to Dagda telling me it was fruitless, and a cold dread settled in my stomach. My hope that we could save Bridget. The pain was evaporating with every minute that ticked by.

I was speeding up time as best as possible without affecting the scene too much. It felt like speeding up Bridget's demise, but I couldn't sit through more of this drivel.

The queen shot me a look of disgust for tampering with her game. She couldn't stop me, nor was she crazy enough to pick a fight with me, but her agitation was evident.

They brought Bridget out finally and I felt rather than saw the recognition register in Declan. He moved imperceptibly, but his breathing picked up.

Like an ice cube in summer, he thawed at an alarming rate, gasping and sputtering with confusion. It was comical to watch truth be told. Or I simply enjoyed my adversary's vulnerabilities.

If adversary were the right word. I had to keep reminding myself that this Bridget wasn't mine.

Well, not totally mine. I'd take part of her.

Blinking rapidly, Declan looked around frantically to place himself, and I understood why. In Puritan clothes and a hot and smelly courtroom was a little unnerving to me and not an average peaceful dreamlike experience for him.

I grabbed his forearm to save him further distress, and he deflated immediately.

"Ruad," he said like a curse.

"Nice of you to join me."

He covered his hand with his mouth as he realized the situation. He was peering at me inquisitively for some sort of explanation of events. I wanted to mouth things to him to mess with him, but I wasn't in a playful enough mood.

"They can't see or hear you. I placed a spell around us," I said in explanation.

"Thank you. What's happening?"

I brought him up to speed on my meeting with Bridget, the allegations that woud happen, and the ones currently happening. Leaving out what I suspected was to happen next.

"And the queen?" he asked when I was done.

Inclining my head in her direction she gave a flirtatious little wave to Declan. She was giddy with the temptation of his presence, dream world or not.

To her, her claiming him was a given. Unfortunately, she might be correct.

He grunted and returned his attention to Bridget, as did I. I couldn't stop the smile that curved my face at seeing her; neither could Declan.

Head held high, shoulders back, she looked more regal than any queen I'd ever seen. "Back down" was not in her vocabulary. She met her opposition with vigor only the fiercest of warriors possessed.

To Bridget, it wasn't about the battle but the war. She searched the crowd as if above them when her eyes met mine.

She let the break in her countenance show for a moment, just a softness in her eyes. A softness and fear.

I winked back at her, delighted in her vulnerability with me and offering her what strength I could. Her slow blink was an acknowledgment of the comfort I offered—her thanks.

I saw the moment her eyes connected with Declan's and him her. The pang of jealousy was lightning quick, but I swallowed it as quickly as it came.

Like a tether connected them, a whole conversation was had in a single glance. I was able to glean enough to know that Bridget recognized him but not to the extent we had hoped. Her thoughts were still muddled, mixing past with the present, still under the queen's influence.

I extended my magic to Bridget to give her a reprieve from her rigidity. She glanced at me when she felt the peace blanket her and her shoulders slumped ever so slightly. The deep breath she took left a small smile on her face directed at me. Take that Declan, I mused.

"She recognizes me but doesn't remember me," he said softly.

"We knew it was a long shot."

And we did, but it didn't make it easier to stomach. The noose was tightening, figuratively and soon literally. Well, it would feel real to Bridget.

"We're staying," I said more in confirmation than a question.

"Aye," he said softly back, never taking his eyes off of Bridget.

I hastened the pace again, now to spare her the extra pain. The rubbish these people had to say about her didn't need to poison her mind. They were careless words uttered by mindless drones, just the queen's playthings. Likely when this debacle had run its course, they would be old ladies plagued by nightmares of their cruelty now. But this was now, and that day may or may not come for them.

That's the brilliance of her madness, rarely lifting a finger herself, sending her comrades to do her dirty work. Charming them with compliments, winning their favor with kindness, and slowly invading their better senses until they were hers.

Eventually, she would discard them, but they didn't know that. No, they thought they were so special to be recognized by her. And in a way they were.

Her usual suspects lacked self-esteem, wanting to fit in with the crowd the queen had trailing her. She was idolized, put on a pedestal, and her victims wanted to be wanted by her.

When they were, they felt as if they were the cream of the crop, except they all felt that way, all of her victims. Until one day the queen disregards them, and they begin to wonder what they did to lose her attention. They fall from her good graces suddenly and think, I must make it right, I must have done something wrong.

And so the queen has them, and she makes them dance for her enjoyment. The more the queen toys with their emotions, the deeper they fall for her trap, the more insidious her plans can become. She preys on their insecurities, their fears, and their hopes, dangling love and appreciation like a carrot on a stick that no one has ever gotten.

That's what the queen does with the mortal men she's able to sway. They're the lucky ones that get the carrot, or so they think, so they're told. The men she dupes are put on the pedestal with her, or so they think. Until the cycle begins again.

Maybe the man hasn't complimented her beauty enough, and they earn her ire. So every day they compliment her from dusk until dawn, and yet she's still upset. Only now it's that they're too suffocating.

Round and round her so-called friends and suitors go. When do they stop? Never.

There's never a moment the queen is content. It's always too much and too little. Hot and cold like a faucet she keeps them swiveling, pivoting, a mass of confusion.

They sputter and stutter. "But I thought that's what you wanted!" they'll cry. To which she derisively snorts how clueless they are, that they never listen, that it's a wonder she still bothers to talk to them at all!

And so begins the discard; the insults are more than the compliments. She cries and cries how horrible they are to her, and they bend until they break, the lucky ones at least.

The unlucky ones, the ones that bend and refuse to break, those she drops ruthlessly. Those ones she's already cried wolf about to anyone that will listen. When those men and women decide that they are the ones that have had enough, they find no comfort in their former friends.

Behind their backs, the queen has begun spinning her web of lies to those closest to them. That way, the cowardly ones think twice before leaving her. They run to their friends in distress and find only malice where they once found understanding.

The cowards run back then and confess their sins as if they were on their death beds. Absolving their crimes while they await their final verdict, heaven or hell. Except there is only hell awaiting them.

She pays her tithe to hell in exchange for more power. Sacrificing her eager followers like lambs to slaughter.

Those that bend but do not break she will try to suck back into her life but those she truly detests. They dared defy her, dared not be enamored with her, dared to think they could live without her. She hurls all of her rage at them until they wish they were dead. Turning their friends into foes, their loved ones suspicious, until they question their sanity.

She does it ruthlessly, without remorse, uncaring of the lives she destroys in the process. She thinks she's Dagda's gift to the world.

That's why she wants Brú na Bóinne, she thinks it's owed her. Her portal to the magical realm to ease her acquisition of mortal men. Why it's practically a gift to the Otherworld! And surely anyone can see that. Or so she thinks.

In reality, her possession of one of the main doors to the Otherworld is like handing a child a knife. A seemingly innocuous object to adults that can cause undue harm to someone that doesn't understand its power. Or tons of harm to someone that does.

Brandishing Brú na Bóinne, the queen would have the ability to decimate the spiritual realm like a plague. Slowly, insidiously, irrevocably, she could introduce a weakness that would extend from the lesser fairies to the more powerful ones and leave us open to attack.

In the Otherworld, like the human realm, there existed different nations and different people. Like the queen had her home among the lesser fairies, Dagda and I shared one, and there were more still. None as loathsome as the Fomorians.

The Nation of Giants rivaled Dagda's reign like no other, and none but them could overthrow his rule. Allowing a fortress like Brú na Bóinne to fall to her hands would be akin to lying down and dying.

Her first order of business would certainly be to unleash the Fomorians and give them the freedom they have long searched for. To conquer and pillage as much as they could lay their hands on, disrupting the lives of the rest of the realm. Thus owing fealty to the queen and advancing her grip on the lesser fairies.

If the queen could control the magical realm likely she would open the portal wide, allowing humans and Fae to mingle again as they had centuries ago. Much to the humans suffering.

Though humans had advanced by leaps and bounds since the days that we coexisted, it would undoubtedly only spread the war that was on the brink. A war that could potentially destroy the human world and undoubtedly make Otherworld bleed.

The Fomorians needed little encouragement to cause mayhem, and after they helped secure the queen's rule in the Otherworld, they would be impossible to stop for the human race. Allowing the queen to have as many human sacrifices as she pleased to increase her power infinitely.

Until she destroyed the human race at least, but that was a while yet.

Her destruction of Bridget and Declan both was just the tip of the iceberg. Anyone that dared defy the queen would be subject to unspeakable cruelty. Only her longing for Lugh, reincarnate or not, kept her from inflicting the worst of her punishment.

With Declan at her side, she could satisfy both the Fae and humans alike. Utterly human, and yet infinitely more, if he fell under her spell, she would have a legitimate claim over both of the realms.

If only Bridget didn't stand in her way. Daughter of Dagda, Brigid was the only one to spoil her plans. It was just a matter of what Dagda would do with her.

Even as I thought that last one, I cringed. It ought to be up to Brigid what she wanted to be done with her life. Just as Bridget had that right. But Dagda was far too powerful, as was his daughter. He had to make the right choice in who would have her hand, what ally was best for the realm.

I was already his ally. And Bridget had already chosen Declan.

Stifling the surge of emotion that threatened to erupt from me like a volcano, I came back to the present. The past was gone, and the future was yet to be made. Though the bitterness of the past lingered with me everywhere I went. I could only hope for a better future now.

And that future started here and now. Except right now, I was just as useless as I had been in the past, and every part of me screamed with the urge to shake Bridget and banish Declan to a dark corner of the universe where the queen couldn't get to him. But that wouldn't stop the queen's advancement; it would only leave the realm wide open to attack.

If I did that, I would spend more energy trying to save Bridget and Declan when together they could take care of themselves. And I would be so busy I would be leaving Dagda vulnerable as well.

It was always a game of chess; move this here, that there, and you'll almost always leave someone important defenseless against an attack. You just had to hope your opponent didn't recognize the weakness before you could assuage it. But you only ever left someone else open.

The plan Dagda had in mind was similarly frustrating. He could shore up one defense while practically handing the other to the queen on a silver platter. I just hoped I could be there to soften the blow.

Entirely like we were now, incapable of helping and yet offering what we could. A wink here, a little protection spell there, giving her some relief from the endless suffering she's had to endure. And will continue to take.

As if on cue, the blows hit devastating proportions when Bridget's father stood up to take the stand. Not Dagda, not by a long shot, but opportunistic all the same. I cast another quick spell over her to save her the worst of it, just a little peaceful magic.

Her eyes met mine, and they were curious to start but turned riotous when she felt the first tendrils of the spell reach her. I don't know what she felt, but she always seemed to know when magic was near, mainly when used on her. She fought the effects, but I insisted, pushing the magic towards her with more effort. I sent her a pleading look that I knew she couldn't ignore. It might not be fair, but it was for her own sake.

She narrowed her eyes at my look, calling me out for my unfairness. But she consented. I inclined my head in thanks, and she numbly nodded back, already in a trance.

Watching the small man's back as he made his way to the stand, I willed myself not to interfere. He wasn't so much trim in stature as he was small in personality, jumping at the chance to make the queen happy.

He deserved the ending he had in store.

And Bridget would hopefully learn her lesson this time, so we didn't have to repeat this one.

As he took his seat, he even looked cowardly, small beady eyes shifting around until they landed on the queen. Her answering nod said, "You know what to do."

My heart shattered when I saw that Bridget had followed the same exchange. Her peace turned volatile until I nudged her with it again. Blinking rapidly at me, she was bewildered and wondered if I had come to the same conclusion she had. I nodded affirmatively.

I turned the questioning out, aware of only Bridget and what I could do for her as her father cried her a witch in front of the judge, jury, and peers. Her flesh and blood had tossed her aside as if she were yesterday's trash, and the queen tomorrow's feast.

That's all her father cared about when he eviscerated his daughter—himself. He cared only about what this situation could do for him. How could he spin it, so he got out without a hitch?

Naturally, he thought his salvation lay with the queen, who had encouraged him down this path—whispering things like how he might be tried a witch if he didn't point his finger at her first. Promising him her hand in marriage, how much he had to look forward to if they could get past this.

He was only too eager to take the bait. To blame his daughter for crimes she hadn't committed. Clear his name to get out of the situation and enjoy his life with his new wife. He deserved it, right? Or so he said.

Luckily the queen would give him exactly what he wanted. And make sure his life was a living hell before being sent straight to torture himself.

All the while, Bridget sat there stone-faced and calm. She was never betraying any emotion or reacting to her father's callous words.

He was calling her a witch, promiscuous, a murderer. Yes, she killed her husband, he would say. Yes, she caused those girls suffering. Yes, she worships the Devil. She talks to a damn bird, too; everyone has seen it indeed.

Bridget never looked at Declan or me. She stared at a point on the wall opposite her, never fidgeting, nor crying, never saying a thing.

While her father buried her alive, she played dead already. She stopped fighting my spell, though she didn't need it much anymore. All of her emotions she had shut off willingly herself, curling inward to protect herself as best she could like she always had. Her abusive husbands had nothing on the abuse her father easily meted her.

The queen, however, fidgeted more by the second. This wasn't what she wanted. Where was the screaming and the shouting? The suffering she so looked forward to.

Bridget's non-reaction was the queen's worst nightmare. How dare Bridget not put on a show for the queen as she should be?

She turned her accusing eyes my way, and I glared back. I stopped the magic surrounding Bridget for long enough to let the queen see for herself that this was all Bridget. I might aid her, but she was in control.

She was in control, a tight control, and she was livid. Her anger fueled her survival and sparked a bit of hope in me.

I realized that while I was so worried about her, she never worried about herself. A blessing and a curse, she never second-guessed her abilities like I was. But she overburdened herself constantly. That was her war, her game of chess. How much pain could she carry before the weight crushed her? Yet, she never has that I've seen. She shored up her vulnerabilities expertly.

I was too busy beaming with pride to notice Declan simmering next to me. He shot to his feet in an instant, marching straight for Bridget's father, ready to throttle him.

Right towards the queen.

The crowd went eerily silent to watch the excitement, but Declan was stopped before he got any closer. A sheriff grabbed him before his fist could connect with her father's jaw. But I wasn't looking at them. I was looking at the queen.

Declan broke my spell when he stood up to launch himself forward, leaving him briefly without my protection. Brief or not, it was just the opening the queen was looking for.

Her magic was off her lips faster than I could blink, and I knew she had planned for a moment such as this. I was kicking myself for letting Declan go after him, for not protecting him better, not warning him. He wasn't prone to outbursts, so I hadn't prepared for that event.

The scene in front of me snapped into order as if nothing had happened. Townspeople resumed their seats, faces blank, attention on Bridget's father. He sat up straight again, no longer shrunken away from the attack.

The main difference was that Declan was now seated next to the queen, a change only the four of us knew. His eyes met mine for a moment before everything changed again.

My eyes took a while to adjust to the sudden brightness of the sun after being in the courtroom. Frantically trying to place my surroundings, I saw the queen front and center with Declan in her thrall, facing a wagon filled with people, maybe three.

They were situated under a large tree, the rope around a thick branch. I knew the scene before I saw the string; I had seen it before more times than I cared to remember. The bitch had what she wanted but was sure to torture us more.

I wasn't sure what spell she had used on Declan, but all of my endeavors to break it proved futile. It was likely because Dagda wanted this result.

She had situated me to the left of them, facing the tree and Bridget's right side, just close enough to see her face filled with terror.

Restrained by two men, Bridget was as disoriented as I had been, and the terror was more severe for the suddenness. I couldn't blame her; she wasn't as cut off from the Spirit world as she had been. The queen couldn't manipulate her memories to the point that she didn't notice anymore.

Declan stared straight ahead as if incapable of looking anywhere else. I saw their eyes meet again, but the only communication between them was dread. He was as unable to help her as she was him.

Their eyes softened, and I looked away, not wanting to spy on their intimate moment before what happened next. And that was the terrifying part. What was the queen's next move?

With Declan under her influence in this dreamscape, she could potentially control his physical body. I was racing through the spells I knew, trying to decipher what was happening to him by the clues it left. There were a few simulating sleepwalking that weren't too difficult to break, but I would need to go now if she had broken the protection on the house, and I wanted to restrain Declan's body and try.

Even if I did, there was no guarantee it wasn't too late. Her changing the scenery felt like it had taken only a second when it could have lasted hours.

The only thing telling me it was alright was Senan's absence. If something were amiss, he would have alerted me. That is if he could.

I was agonizing over what to do when Dagda came to mind again. This was a part of his plan, shitty though it was. But the queen might have seen through to his plan and made alternate ones.

That was the scary part, the part of the game that you could never fully account for. No matter how many times you played poker with someone, there's still the chance that they've figured you out too. That you've given your hand, and you didn't even know they saw right through you.

If the plan goes the way Dagda thinks it will, we'll be on home turf, back on our side of the dream world of Otherside.

That's if it goes that way.

In the event the queen has us figured out, there's no telling what way this will go. Bridget could die here but never awaken anywhere else. She might die in the real world, too, and what does the queen care if she's already secured Declan?

The possibilities kept my feet firmly planted where they were. Senan should have the capability to prevent the queen from abducting Declan's physical body if she was using a sleepwalking spell. And if not, Dagda might not let me, anyway.

I only hoped my presence here would help Bridget hold on to that shred of hope she had found. Fixing my gaze on Bridget, she tore hers away from Declan to give me a small, sad smile. She may recognize him, but I was the one that had been by her side, proved my mettle.

At least in these last few days, that is. In their world, it was him who had been there for her. And that was why I had to make sure he got back to her after this was over.

The men surrounding Bridget had completed their task, and each stood back to survey their handiwork. Thick rope wrapped securely around her slender neck, laying heavily on her broad shoulders. Her breathing was erratic, and even the spell for peace I had placed on her did little to ease the terror.

Having had enough of the theatrics, I used a different, much stronger charm than I had been, and her face went blissfully blank. Similar to the type of magic the queen was using on Declan, this separated her from this reality.

I sent her to a favorite haunt of mine, a place in the woods that was peaceful and quiet, a book in her hands. That much I could do for her.

If looks could kill, the queen would have struck me dead. I vanished as the rope pulled tight.

PART TWO

CHAPTER 1

I was back in the woods outside of Declan's manor in an instant, but I couldn't drag myself in the house yet. My mouth was dry, and my heart was thundering in my ears. Bending over at the waist, I sat down instead, my legs quivering before giving out.

Nausea roiled in my stomach, and I knew I had to get ahold of myself quickly, but I couldn't stop. Panting and shaking, I lay flat on my back, taking gulping breaths of the cool air to cool the sweat that had broken out on my skin.

Something wet and warm was on my face, and I threw myself to a sitting position in my panic. Failinis was standing over me, tongue still lolling out of his mouth. He must have run here once I popped in; he was as out of breath as I was. I was a little unnerved. I hadn't even noticed his approach when I had to lay down against the influx of nausea that hit me.

The dog placed his giant head on my chest, and I wrapped my arms around him, anchoring my swirling emotions. He stayed there patiently while I grappled with sickness.

I wasn't sure if Bridget was alive or not. Salem may have been a reenactment of the events that had taken place, but whether they were only in Bridget's head or if her body had swung from that tree as she had all those years ago, I wasn't sure.

Or if the queen had killed her once she had Declan.

Of all of her deaths, that one continued to be the worst. Seeing someone you love strung up like a deer, her face purpled, tongue swelling, grasping at the rope secured around her slim neck.

That was the first I had observed from that close, usually spying from beyond the portal. I didn't need to stick around to see the end up close. It was burned in my mind.

Slowly I mastered my senses, but I had no energy to move. No desire to. I stared at the trees and the sky beyond near comatose, dreading the task that lay ahead of me.

I couldn't *feel* her. She felt like a redwood tree. Bold and beautiful, sturdy and scarred, that ancient wisdom you felt that whispered to you in the forest.

Usually, I had a sense of her, just a peaceful presence in my bones. A tether forged between us when the world was new.

I was frantically tugging on that connection, spinning round and round in my selfish despair. I'm not sure how much time I wasted on my agony when a dragonfly landed on Failinis' snout.

So innocuous, the dragonfly was perched just longer than seemed natural—a breath past a rest. But I didn't need the extra nudge; I knew it for the sign that it was.

And I felt peaceful.

CHAPTER 2

When Ruad vanished, so did we. I wasn't at all convinced it would work, but I had to do something.

It was better than twiddling my thumbs while I watched Bridget struggle for air.

I was afraid the queen's magic would work on me or that she would know it hadn't. It was a gamble, but it was what I had to work with.

I felt guilty for lying to Ruad and Senan, but they had to believe it too. The runes my mother was instructed to draw on me once I had taken the tea were to prevent possession specifically. And any other form of mind control. It wasn't that I didn't trust their magic per se, but it made me feel a modicum of control.

So in the brief moment that both men were occupied with me, she scrambled to draw them on my chest. The warding we had been using was good enough for evil spirits and lesser fairies as Carman and her sons had been.

But a power like the queen required something more substantial. And I couldn't risk anyone giving me away. Especially not myself.

I felt the first flicker of her magic when I had rushed Bridget's father. It beckoned to me in a way Ruad's never could.

While Ruad's felt earthy and calm, the queen shot wild and vicious. Hers was greedy, while he was generous. It practically begged me to let it take over, or else. I had the feeling that if Ruad had tried the same thing, I would hardly know anything had happened. I'd have consented like it *was* what I wanted.

The spell work that Ruad had used around us had felt different, like the protections weren't triggered. It blanketed me like a warm breeze.

When the queen used her spell, I felt the print of the runes on my chest burning. They repelled the magic like the two opposing sides of a magnet.

The spell pushed as hard as it could, but it was never going to get through, and I sighed inwardly in relief. It was a risky plan without the approval of the supernatural experts at my disposal but a necessary one.

Not risking looking at her to see if she had noticed, I walked to her side, hoping that was the directive. Once beside her, I gauged her reaction momentarily before she poofed us somewhere else.

CHAPTER 3

Racing in the house, slightly delirious, I fell to my knees when I saw Declan's body still prone on the couch. I could've smacked the man, but he wouldn't feel it, which would be wasted.

And I didn't want to do that in front of Joan.

"He's still here," I breathed.

Though I looked at Joan, it was Senan that answered.

"Och, aye, and where would he have gone?"

He was a little irritated, and I got up from the floor.

"I'm sorry I frightened you all. It's just that the queen got Declan, and I was afraid she had already taken him to the portal."

There was something queer about the look on Joan's face as she fidgeted with the hem of her sleeve.

"Joan?" I questioned.

"He didn't want you to know in case," she said.

"In case what? What didn't he want me to know?"

"Well, he's only pretending to be under her spell. And yours. While you were both there with him, he had me add to the wardings on him,"

"To what end? She could have killed Bridget then! As she very well may still!" I roared a little louder than I wished.

Joan didn't deserve my anger; Declan did.

"Yes, we know. He knows. But if the queen got distracted by him, maybe she'd forget to keep torturing Bridget. She couldn't kill her before she knew she had Declan there physically. So he's buying you some time for you to sneak in and get her."

"That was his backup plan if she didn't wake up and get herself out."

"She didn't then?"

"She's not entirely under the queen's influence anymore, so that's a massive step in the right direction. The trouble is the confusion. It's like those moments after a nightmare when you can't figure out what is real yet. Her memories are fragmented, tainted by the memories the queen implanted,"

"And is she...did she..." Brian choked on the words, but I knew the rest of the question.

"Yes. And no,"

"But she's alive?" Joan this time.

"Yes, but I don't know how she is or what the queen is planning next, not exactly," I amended.

Joan rushed to me, wrapping her arms as far around me as possible. I was taken aback at her openness, still more used to the wariness of her fellow relatives.

Truth be told, I needed that hug more than I would like to admit. Returning the embrace, I thanked her quietly, and the tears in her eyes made mine well up as well.

I released her before I caved to that tsunami of emotion that hit me. Shaking my head softly, I blinked back the tears and squared my shoulders for some false bravado.

"That must have been difficult," she whispered.

"Every time," I said.

Her eyes widened before she squeezed my hand once in silent understanding. The approval of a human woman had never meant more to me besides Bridget.

"So, how will we get her?" she said, back to business.

"That is the question."

CHAPTER 4

While my eyes adjusted to the brightness, I stared straight ahead, seeing nothing. But when I was staring directly into Bridget's eyes, I almost blew my cover.

Swallowing the alarm, it took everything in me not to jump on that wagon and destroy anyone that tried to stop me. But it wouldn't help her. It was pretend.

It had to be.

My emotions warred with each other, reality warped. It was real, and it wasn't. But what if it was?

We were in the Otherworld, but we weren't. I wasn't physically. Bridget was.

Where the queen could make us see whatever she wanted but what might all be a mirage. Or not.

Like a green screen, she could be Bridget right now, in the flesh. All of the surroundings save the tree and the rope, a figment of imagination. The rope could tighten, and Bridget would perish, and I could stop it right now.

Or I would lunge for her and grasp only air. Ghost as I was in this dreamscape, maybe I couldn't.

The plan hinged on the queen's ego. Is she sure enough that she had me? Sure enough to eliminate the bait before securing me?

So I gritted my teeth and did nothing. The plan was to buy Ruad time and do some recon myself. Hopefully, the queen would lead me right to where she had Bridget.

And hopefully, Bridget was alive.

The worst part of this plan was that I had no exit strategy. I was at Ruad's mercy for that. Which I begrudgingly was faithful in.

I wanted to say the man was a fox, but I got a distinct impression that he had moxie. In my experience, a man that had as strong a sense of self as he did it was usually because he had nothing to hide. And he didn't hold any punches.

Which, I hate to admit, I admired. I looked up to even. Too many people crumbled at adversity, changed their stories when the going got tough.

Ruad never flinched, never balked, looked me straight in the eye even though he was in love with Bridget too. I couldn't help but respect him.

And so I trusted him with my life, literally. There was no better man to go into battle with, even if my death would benefit him.

That part struck a chord a little. But in my younger years, I would have died for less. Ready to go to war over a sideways glance.

At least this would be an honorable death.

The rope was fastened to the executioner's delight at long last, and I dug my fingers into my palm to keep myself planted. Like the tree she'd swing from, I couldn't move, couldn't break under pressure.

Bridget's face turned peaceful before Ruad vanished with a last vile glare at the queen. If he could do that the whole time I wondered why we were in this mess. But I believed he had his reasons. I felt the pull of his magic try to take me with him, but it didn't work. The queen's greedy hold on me was more substantial.

I made a mental note to ask him about the intricacies of their realm later. There were rules and exceptions I had trouble making sense of.

Once Ruad had vanished, the rope snapped tight. And still, I stared.

CHAPTER 5

"The trouble with saying she's at Brù na Bóinne is like saying she's in New York City. It's a great starting point but *where*? There's Manhattan, the Bronx, Queens, millions of apartments and storefronts and *places* she could be," I started.

"She could be in a closet in the Guggenheim, and I would never know because she's been warded against my magic finding her."

"The pendant we used earlier wouldn't work?" Joan queried.

"It might give us a good starting point, but I'd still have to do a lot of footwork that way. That's why I was hoping something would wake her up. If I could at least see what she sees through our bond, I might be able to place her. And she'd have a fighting chance of getting herself out if she wasn't spelled."

I heaved a sigh. I knew everything, but I was poring through my knowledge and coming up short. There were ways to break the spell in person, but that's the beauty of taking her. All of those ways required her physical body, tonics and herbs, and the like. A strand of her hair maybe would work if I could find one.

The wardings were the other obstacle. Some spells could work like a bomb, hurtling it in a direction that could obliterate the magic holding her captive.

But there were things in the Otherworld that I would risk releasing. Things that made the queen look like the Queen of England.

The specific magic that could free her required me to isolate the magic from her. So round and round we went there.

Dagda could free her with a snap of his fingers but for a price. A price steeper than I was willing to pay.

And a decision I wasn't willing to make for her.

The inevitability simmered just below the surface, ratcheting my frayed nerves to a fever pitch. If I played my cards right, we could avoid the outcome I feared. But every second that ticked by filled my veins with a blackness so thick it obscured thought.

I needed to think; I couldn't afford to succumb to the darkness growing inside of me. I'd spent centuries in that void, unfeeling, unthinking, barely more than a corpse. Feeling like that now was only giving up.

A small hand on my forearm broke me from my spiral. I must have looked like the ghost I'd been these last centuries because Joan's eyes were wide with shock.

"I'm sorry," I said softly.

I summoned a map of Brú na Bóinne, a rendering that shifted as the city did. Every brick added and removed was accounted for in real-time, making the map look like a confusing etch-a-sketch.

And my task even more complicated.

The thriving metropolis was squarely situated on the other side of the portal through Brù na Bóinne. Like Ellis Island to New York City, it was only one entry point to a land and people more complex than could be understood in words.

And perfect for the portal it was, used for trade and travel like any port city in the mortal world, still to this day. Lesser fairies required the magic of the doorway to jump between worlds, while the more formidable fairies were forbidden to. And humans, when our kinds had frequently intermingled.

That was put to an end by Dagda's reign when the humans began advancing faster with the technology we had taught them when they started using it against us. And the Fomorians swore to end the humans.

That peace existed for thousands of years, the Fomorians cowed by the might of Dagda's court, lesser fairies content to remain in the Otherworld. A peace the queen has long wanted to shatter.

That Declan would help her complete.

And Bridget might be able to prevent.

"You can see why this was not my first resort," I said, referencing the map as it shifted like sand in the ocean.

Snapping my fingers, I showed them every living creature in that city as they went about their lives. Like a *Where's Waldo* book, creatures big and small moved to and fro at a relentless pace, in every direction possible.

Used to find fleeing subjects, this map was invaluable. You could ward against the map, but the average criminal wasn't likely to bother, driven by impulse and not careful planning. The queen was not acting on impulse.

"The city of Tír Tairngire," I said with a sweep of my hand, inviting them closer.

Moving closer Joan placed a hand to her mouth, agape with wonder. But it was Brian who spoke.

"Surely, it's not that big."

"Bigger. Tír Tairngire, or the promised land, is one of many cities in the Otherworld, with everything imaginable in between. Towns and rivers, oceans and deserts, every creature from your nightmares and ones so horrible no human has laid eyes on. At least not to tell the tale.

"Like a twin of your world only much more magical. And much scarier."

"I see," was all Joan said through the hand still covering her mouth.

"Yes, we are more civilized than we were centuries ago when most of your stories were originated, as are you. Bridget could be anywhere in or under the city. Most of our cities have matching cities underground to accommodate some of those more sinister fairies, the ones that prefer darkness and chaos.

"The Gauls called them Albios or heaven, Bitu for the mortal world, and Dubnos or hell."

I snapped another map next to the one on the table, a black replica almost identical. The main difference was the fairies walking around, much more significant than the ones aboveground and with more teeth typically.

"If I had to guess, the queen has her underground. While Dagda may be the official ruler of the realm, ones like the queen who *chafe* against his rule reside underground. By choice or happenstance, a general predisposition to be disagreeable, or a combination of all of the above, I couldn't tell you.

"There are those like the queen and the Fomorians that have plotted against him for millennia. And those foul beasts stay in their underground world, trading only with those aboveground for supplies they need, being banned from the mortal realm.

"When Carman and her sons resurfaced, I was sent to investigate and intervene if necessary. I knew of Bridget and Declan and had kept tabs on them, but the attack on Brian was the evidence I needed to get involved.

"That Carman and her sons had been resurrected *and* in the mortal world was a mystery at the time. Only a handful of fairies, or Fae since we're talking collectively now, are capable of breaking through the warding. That it was done secretly is even more concerning.

"That's where Senan came in. Clurichaun are leprechauns, except they're usually drunk. That's the only distinction. Both hoard treasure, like the runed spear, and both can pop in and out of realms like the sprites.

"They understand the wards because they are a part of it. Their magic is tied to it. When Bridget went to get the spear, she was in a part of the Otherworld. A small part, remnants of a deserted town like the human one established near it.

"And when the queen came for her, we knew we had our culprit, though we suspected already. If Dagda is the king aboveground, she is the underground queen.

"Like an illegal organization, we have put up with her because she is the evil we know. Power leaves a vacuum, and with her usurped, there's no telling who would replace her. But her friends are vast and powerful.

"This *slight* is the worst committed by her in centuries and will be remedied. But I tell you this because the remedy is war.

"Unless, *unless,* we can get Bridget out and keep Declan from her grip. But I don't know if that is possible."

When I returned my gaze to the couple, their hands were grasped. Though they each looked a little pale, the steel in their eyes told me everything I needed to know. They weren't going to back down from a fight.

"We're going to use the pendant to locate approximately where she is. *But,* and this is a big one, I may need Declan as bait."

CHAPTER 6

I didn't know if my breathing would give me away or not, but it was all I could do to keep from puking. I was going to faint if I had to look at the face of the woman I loved turn purple for one more second.

The queen didn't seem to notice as she whisked us away. This time I felt it, like swimming in the ocean when the waves push and pull while you're underwater.

We landed somewhere new, a living room. Dark wood floors met warm reds and browns between the Victorian and Middle Ages, torture devices included. Shackles adorned chairs, maces, swords, and daggers decorated one wall. A fire burned in the hearth nearly the size of the wall it adorned.

Brown hair graced the black leather sofa facing the roaring fire, a slim hand beckoning me forward. My stomach turned, instincts sounding the alarm, but I took the steps required until I met the face that belonged to the hair barely peeking over the top of the couch.

My heart lurched as my eyes met with Bridget's, but I willed my features to surprised delight. Mouth dry, I blinked quickly while I assessed the situation. This couldn't be *her*.

But I think I wasn't supposed to know that.

Words failed me, but I forced myself to say something, anything.

"Bridget," was all I could manage.

Her saccharine smile made the hairs on my neck stand up. Bridget wasn't prone to smiling like that. If she'd furrowed her brow, I might have been more inclined to believe her.

Moving closer, I still wasn't sure what I was supposed to be, how I was supposed to behave. Did I miss her? Was she never missing? This ruse would be up soon if I didn't act right.

Seating myself beside her in front of the blaze, I felt the wrongness of her like a cold wind. This close, her eyes hid none of the madness that lurked beneath, and it was an effort not to run.

I felt like a fly in a spider's web. Trapped, watching the predator stalk closer, incapable of escaping.

But she *smelled* like Bridget. Like chamomile shampoo and rain on a warm breeze. I broke eye contact briefly, the quiet stretching on interminably, to notice her outfit.

There was a stain on her black button-down shirt. A stain I remembered from the bus bucket I had wrenched from her that last night at work.

She always insisted on carrying them herself, because she could, because it wasn't my job, it was hers. Especially at the end of the night when customers were gone, it was the last one of the night.

I know because I had a matching stain on my shirt that night. Pasta sauce had overflowed the bowl it was in, the dish on the top.

She had fought me on it. But I had won, spilling sauce on each of us in the process. Because she was always too stubborn for her own good.

The shirt the selkie had taken from her at my house. Before we'd ever come to Ireland.

The first lick of genuine terror hit me then, and I prayed she couldn't scent it. She wasn't just pretending to be Bridget to get me.

I think she wanted to *be* Bridget, which was a whole different level of insanity. She wanted what Bridget had and felt she lacked.

I wondered how much her desire to be the queen of the Otherworld weighed against her longing for Bridget's life. And whether those two intertwined.

All that time, I sat and pondered. The twisted grin never faltered, her eyes shining with the same eerie glow; I wasn't sure if she had blinked once.

It was mere seconds, but a few seconds too many. My suspicions confirmed I debated how to play this.

"What happened to your shirt?" I said.

It was a good enough place to start. The trance was broken; she looked down to see the week-old sauce on her shirt, looking back at me perplexed.

"You spilled that on me, remember? Fifty-three's mussels?"

"When?"

"Tonight, silly," she said playfully, placing a hand on my arm.

She might have the facts straight, alarmingly so, but Bridget never called anyone silly. Kids maybe not adults.

"Oh, right," was all I said.

So she wants to go back to that night? Why? To erase everything that had happened since? Or because that was the first time we had kissed. Well, the real Bridget and me.

Dredging up that memory brought a mess of emotions with it. There was something different once I had her in my home, in my space. Something primal.

That protectiveness I felt for her was replaced by rage at the impersonator in front of me. Because of this psychopath in front of me, my Bridget was in danger. What kind of danger I still wasn't sure. Judging by my surroundings, the queen had an imagination for terrorizing people.

My Bridget.

But why didn't the queen make it look like my living room? Unless it was a weird loophole in the enchantment. Or better

124

yet, a subtle threat I was supposed to acknowledge to ensure I played whatever sick game she was getting at. It worked.

"Why don't you get more comfortable?" I hedged like I had the night Bridget had slept in my arms.

Engulfed by my clothes, it was a testament to my willpower that I didn't tear them off her. But I was only getting used to seeing her that way myself. Before then, I was always attracted to her, but that night was like a switch went off.

I wasn't just attracted to her physically anymore; it was the whole package. Every fiery inch of her. My own little fairy.

This abomination wasn't her.

But she still stared at me, unblinking.

"Aren't you going to get me some clothes?"

"Of course," I said, standing in one fluid motion.

I didn't know where she was going with this one, but I stalked off to where I could only assume the bedroom was. Glad to leave her creepy ass on the couch.

Except she got off the couch with me, following behind me soundlessly. I only noticed her when I turned the couch corner to head back to where a staircase wound its way up. Fuck.

I needed time, time to figure out her end goal here. Time for Ruad to do something.

The stairs were massive, leaving the living room, a large foyer to the left. Dominated by ornate wooden double doors, a chandelier, and a round table with a vase of dead flowers in it, the foyer faced the stairs and two hallways leading behind on either side. Directly across from the living room I was in was a massive dining room, the long table as intricately carved as the front doors.

I continued, reminding myself not to gape; I think I wasn't supposed to notice it. Heading up the stairs, the thick red carpet under my feet muffled any noise, furthering the creep vibes even more. It was like a vampire's lair; I was waiting to see a coffin in the room.

At the top of the stairs, I went left, picking the first door I saw. It wasn't at all situated like any of my homes, so I wondered why she made it seem like I should know the way.

I'd guessed right, I think. A bed dwarfed the room, complete with gauzy drapes around the four-post bed. It wasn't a coffin, but it followed suit with the color scheme, blood-red and black everywhere.

Two armoires were on either wall, one in front of me and one on the right. The one on the right was taller, so I ventured there. Opening the drawers I kept my t-shirt and sweatpants in, I was appalled to find my actual clothes in the drawers.

The clothes that remained in my New Jersey home that had been washed and folded and put back by one of my assistants. I pulled out the pair I had given to Bridget that night, handing them over, glad my hands weren't shaking as much as I thought they would be.

It was unnerving. My discomfort multiplied when the queen took off her clothes right there in front of me—watching as she unveiled Bridget's body, wrapped in lacey things I had purchased for her in Ireland.

Something must have shown on my face because her disappointment was palpable. Schooling my features, I knew it was too late; I'd offended her.

"What? I thought you liked her body?"

Shit.

CHAPTER 7

The pendant swiveled at the end of the chain in a dizzying dance. Much faster than before, as if it too were struggling to find her.

Maybe it was.

It went faster and faster, angrily swirling over the underground map. Finally, it froze over the cave system to the west, the entrance to Dubnos.

Damn.

"What do you know of Tech Duinn?"

"The House of Donn, where souls go over by Bull Rock."

I merely stared at Joan; she was an encyclopedia of Irish mythology. She shrugged in response.

"Saves me time. Yes, precisely. Specifically, where departed souls go, the underworld. Or hell, if that's what you prefer,

"The queen has a long history with Donn, trading the souls of her mortal victims for power; many of those souls still reside there, tortured and deranged. If Bridget is there, our lousy luck has gotten worse.

"Like the Greek myth, when the man went to bring his wife back from Hades and was told not to look back, but he did? And then his wife had to spend half of the year with Hades? The same concepts apply here.

"Most of what humans have dealt with are fairies and sprites, lesser beings with minor magic. Bridget's brought out the heavy hitters. The ruling Fae has dictated the laws of nature since this world was created. But they always have these absurd rules, twisted bargains, loopholes.

"If the queen has bargained with Donn, using Bridget's soul, it will take a miracle to get her out. This tells us that Carman and her sons were likely a part of that agreement, their souls for Bridget's. But why?"

I started pacing as I thought. Carman was valuable to Donn; before she was sent to her death, she had brought him countless souls. But her soul was worth as much in the underworld as it was in the mortal realm. She was a valuable instrument of torture.

But Donn had to know Dagda would never allow her to remain. And the queen knew so too. So it was like lending her but for what gain?

Dagda wouldn't let Bridget remain in hell. Except to be reincarnated.

But this is all unnecessary if the queen never gets Declan. So what am I missing?

Unless the queen has something on Dagda, or Dagda had set this up from the start. To prevent Brigid and Lugh from claiming his throne rightfully.

Maybe he *wants* the queen to get Declan, who has the blood of the Fomorians flowing through his veins. So he can attach Bridget to a Fomorian of his choosing.

To protect his claim to the throne.

Because if his daughter were linked with Lugh, no one in the realm would argue their rule. But that's if he made them immortal.

Giving them to the queen gives him what he wants without getting his hands dirty. The queen gets Declan, but that won't matter if he marries Bridget to the Fomorian prince.

He gets a son-in-law that no Fae or fairy would accept as their ruler but pacifies the Fomorians. A daughter cowed into submission.

The queen gets a new toy for however long she wants, gaining more power or simply something to entertain her.

And I was so lost in my misery I never put the pieces together. Or better yet, killed in the process.

So Dagda had allowed Carman to be freed to draw me out, knowing I couldn't sit back and let Bridget handle her alone. Knowing I could stand in between Bridget and Declan.

Knowing that the only time I ever had Bridget in my lifetime was when she married that dreaded giant. And I'd taken the bait.

CHAPTER 8

I stuttered.

"Whose?" I said, genuinely confused. It was the only answer that gave me an out, anyway.

"Bridget's, but if you would prefer someone else, I can do that," she said.

"Um..."

She shimmered like heat off the blacktop on the hottest day of the year before reappearing as she was during Bridget's trial. Like the woman from Salem, Mary, I think it was.

It was an improvement not to have to look at Bridget's face, but I couldn't say I found this woman to be attractive. She seemed to notice that and bore a resemblance to Bridget again but changed her features slightly to make it not Bridget.

A chill ran through me.

"Why don't you show me you?"

She frowned at that. Like I'd insulted her.

"Why be me when I can be whomever and whatever I want?" she said with a purr.

And again, she changed, wavy lines of magic blurring her features until she was taller and leaner. And much closer to me.

She ran a hand seductively down from my collarbone to the middle of my chest as she took another long stride forward until her breath warmed the air between us. Looking through her lashes at me, she reached out with her other hand to grasp my waist, but I twisted out of her reach.

Her eyes turned feline, genuinely feline, with slits for pupils instead of the round ones she had a moment ago. Baring her now sharp teeth, she closed the distance between us with a pull of my shirt until her lips were inches from mine.

130

"Why aren't you obeying?" she spat.

I felt the licks of her magic claw against the markings on my chest. Sharp talons digging for my psyche, meeting a brick wall.

"What did you do?" she screeched, using genuine claws to tear through my shirt.

Her fingertips curved inward in predatory spikes, leaving my shirt in ribbons. And though they'd met with flesh, the skin underneath hadn't so much as reddened.

The waves became tendrils of smoke, black and oily, slithering toward me. Her hair transformed to match it as if it were the dark magic now reaching for me, her teeth sharpening and lengthening like the panther she now resembled.

"Clever," she snarled, running her hands lower until I swatted them away in irritation.

She smirked as those snakes of mist curled around me, testing me, tasting me, probing for weakness. They slithered up my bare chest, coiling around my back and up my neck to my ears as if searching for a way in.

Chills raced across my spine as goosebumps danced on my skin. Like thousands of ants marched on the hairs on my body, their touch feather-light and *creepy.*

I refused to react beyond the physical response my body gave: no smirks or scowls, nothing. My face was made of granite as those tickly wisps covered me thoroughly.

Our eyes were locked in a match of wills. Each of us waiting for the other to cave first. She did.

As her magic licked across my skin, she snarled in frustration at last. Those tiny ants became fire ants, and with each lick across my skin, I felt the flames burn hotter but not enough to do damage—much to her chagrin.

"Ethniu," she said like a curse.

I didn't dare react.

"Your mother, or didn't your dear pal tell you?"

The confusion shone in my eyes involuntarily.

"Yes, that dear friend of yours that stepped out of the way for you? Who let you have the woman he loves?"

She sauntered across the room like the jungle cat she was, quiet and deadly—black smog in her wake. A tantalizing smile graced her lips as she strolled to the bed, pushing back the curtain to seat herself. I had to turn to face her, placing my back to the drawers full of my clothes.

"You didn't think he was indeed on your side? How silly. Surely a man like you doesn't have to reduce himself to someone else's sloppy seconds?"

If steam could curl out of my ears like the old cartoons, I'm sure it would be by now. But still, I remained stoic, crossing my arms over my nearly bare chest and leaning against the dresser. I knew what she was doing, and I wasn't going to bite.

"No, a man like you could have any woman he wanted: red hair and all. You have it all, looks, brawn, and brains. And let's not forget that hint of *something* no one could ever quite put their finger on. That magic that courses through your veins. Your extensive veins, in those extra-large arms, fill out your monstrous frame. Have you never wondered why you settled for *her*?" She spat the last.

I'm not going to take the bait, I reminded myself. It wasn't worth it. She was all talk; Ruad was working on getting me out right this second.

But he did love her.

"Have you never noticed the strings they pulled? Never questioned why you were here? You, instead of him? How can you be sure you acted on your own free will and not by a spell he'd placed on you? Her too? Just toying with you, using you as their willing sacrifice?"

Gritting my teeth, I could feel the scowl deepening of its own accord. I could feel magic, I reminded myself. I'd know if I were under a spell. And Ruad has never been anything less than honorable.

Except maybe for kissing her. And her him. That time in the bathroom...

"It's a weird game they have been playing for millennia. Right now, I'm sure they're laughing at you from the bedroom. How blindly you ate what they shoveled your way, begging for more. Thanking *her* and the stars above for giving her to you. While she slowly sucked the life right from you, without you even noticing.

"And then they dump you at my doorstep to be wiped from existence and trapped for eternity in this wasteland like me. Getting power from your suffering."

She would never. Could never. Could Ruad?

"Big, strong, handsome, intelligent, and *gullible*. You knew she was too good to be true, and yet you ignored that feeling. Instead, you saw a victim, a damsel in distress. She played you like a fiddle, every forlorn look, every night clinging to you like a sad puppy, even the circles under her eyes. Like a moth to a flame, she lured you in, calling on your need to be the hero, to sacrifice yourself for *her.*"

She stood from the bed, gliding to where I stood in three long strides. Bracing herself against me with those hands on my chest, no longer bearing claws but dainty polished fingers that curled into my bare chest, lighting up the wardings drawn there.

"We could fight them, you and me. You don't have to be their whipping post. I could help you if it weren't for these things."

Idly tracing the wardings as she spoke, they shone like embers in the night. I was inclined to believe the wardings,

burning hotter with every stroke of her hand as if to turn her to
ash.

"What about my mother?" I growled, voice coming out
hoarser than I thought.

"She's a witch. Why do you think she knows so much about
us? How she can do magic of this caliber?"

She was lying. This was all to get me to give in, to take her
side.

"She's no better than the other two, you know," she
whispered.

Pushing off of the dresser, I shook away those greedy
hands, stalking off to where I didn't know but away from her.
The door slammed in my face before I could get to the hallway,
whipping my head around in a rage.

My hand was on the dresser, shoving with all my might
when I felt it. It felt like sugar dissolving in coffee, a melting
sensation, sand through an hourglass.

It stopped the war I was about to wage, the temper that
burned rational thought in a white-hot blaze. It fizzled out like
a firework, there one second and gone the next.

I felt a moment of disbelief; it had been years since I felt out
of control like this. The anger that used to be a second skin
wielded whether necessary or not. She had done this to me,
this *thing* in front of me.

Turning to her, the smile that split her face in half was
nothing short of vile. She pointed at her chest with that vicious
sparkle in her eyes until I looked down at my own; the
wardings were gone.

I could barely hear the dresser as it crashed to the ground,
splintering wood, and sending shards flying dangerously
through the room.

CHAPTER 9

"Take the wardings off, all of them," I ordered Joan.

She flinched at my tone, and I winced.

"But won't she be able to control him then?" she whispered, cringing slightly.

I made an effort to relax my shoulders and take a few calming breaths before answering. I didn't want to scare the poor woman. I hadn't noticed the thunder cloud of anger wrapped around me. Once I saw her reaction, I felt it suffocating me, threatening to pull me down.

Like he'd anticipated it doing.

"Sorry, better?" I asked Joan before proceeding.

She relaxed her shoulders in response, rolling them backward out of the hunched position she had been in. Blowing out a breath of air, she nodded her affirmative. I cast a spell of silence around us before I began.

"This goes deeper than I had thought," I started. "It's all a ruse—a wild goose chase.

"The queen will get Declan, or we won't get Bridget. It was always going to culminate at this moment. We can save some of the melodrama by letting her control him for now. It buys us some time.

"Dagda, the all-father," I hedged, they nodded their understanding, and I continued.

"Dagda rules all of the Otherworld. He relishes his position. We've known something was amiss for a while. Carman and her sons haven't been in Bitu for thousands of years, for a good reason.

"Unless they were let out. Maybe they were let out to lure me in. To get Bridget in Ireland, where so many portals exist. So the queen could capture her.

"I thought it was so the queen could get to Declan, and that's partially true. But maybe it's to keep Bridget from getting Declan. To keep them apart. Joan, why would Dagda want to do that?" I asked, feeling like a teacher in a classroom.

Biting her lip, she answered almost guiltily.

"Because he's a Fomorian."

Brian looked at her perplexed, urging her to go on.

"Legend goes that my great-great-great-grandfather was a Fomorian. Probably more greats are necessary, but you get the idea.

"Some time in the Middle Ages, the Fae were summoned to help deal with the plagues that tore through Europe. Their aid came with a price.

"Before the portals were closed, before we forsook our worship of the Fae as Gods and made bargains with the fairies, there were some misunderstandings between humans and Fae.

"Well, there always were, but the stakes got higher. The more humans asked for, the more convoluted the agreements became. More loopholes were integrated into these bargains both by fairies and humans alike. So they ceased comingling. But the high Fae particularly disagreed with this, the more sinister ones to be exact.

"They'd come up with a solution of sorts. A loophole. The fairies had long wanted half-human children. Some for love, for fun, what have you. A lot of fairies and humans were together when the world was new.

"Once the portal was closed, many believed these half-fae could jump between worlds as quickly as the leprechauns. Being of both worlds, the enchantments wouldn't be able to stop them; they were designed to keep out the strongest of the

136

fairies. Half-human hybrids were barely a blip on the radar, just like the harmless sprites, nymphs, and leprechauns.

"It seems backward, but it's the cunning of their magic that allows them to pop back and forth, their magic not being as tremendous is their advantage. Like leaving the back door open, if it was necessary to interact with humans, Dagda had to permit the wee folk to continue.

"But the wee folk lacking in great power are incredibly crafty. Any strong Fae in the Otherworld that tried to strike a bargain with a leprechaun usually found themselves out of their bargaining chip and without their promised treasure. But half-humans were the alternative, their sons and daughters sent to do their bidding.

"There were fae-humans before the realms were closed, but wherever they called home, they were made to stay, memories wiped of their mixed nature. It made life easier for them that way.

"When the high Fae were called in for aid, it was the half-breeds that did the summoning. The human race was brought to their knees in despair from the disease that went rampant around their world. They begged, and Dagda agreed as they were Fae too.

"His asking price was the dismissal of their magic. If they could summon the Fae, they posed a threat to the realm. He saw the danger in their unwitting magic.

"But a few of those more dangerous Fae slipped through with Dagda when he crossed realms. One of whom was a great beast of a man, Balor.

"Balor made a few deals of his own. One of which was with a mortal woman, my grandmother, a couple of generations removed. It's said that in exchange for a son she asked for knowledge about the future. She wanted to protect herself and her children, so she wanted knowledge of wars and famines

137

before they happened, so she knew which kings to follow or crops to grow.

"Dagda was already caring for the disease that prevailed. She had borne no children by her husband, but the giant favored her. He gifted her nothing more than intuition, but it was infallible. Intuition in exchange for a baby. When she bore him a son, she knew he would come calling for him before long, thanks to her intuition.

"So she prepared her son from a young age, currying favor with the most skilled swordsmen in the land to train him. And when Balor came, at last, to claim his son, having left a backdoor open, he was slain by his son.

"Upon hearing of this, Dagda called after Balor's son and finding him an agreeable sort, he allowed him to remain in Bitu. He had done Dagda a favor in eliminating Balor and doubly for exposing a weakness in the barrier. As thanks, he also allowed their magic to remain so long as they used it for good.

"Since then, the women in my line have often been wise women, spiritual leaders, and healers. And the men have been prominent in stature with a magic of their own. Some call it charisma or charm, influence, but they have an inner wisdom that is centuries old."

"Why have you never mentioned this before?" Brian queried.

"You always laugh at me and my stories. And besides, it was only a legend. A story my mother had told me and her mother before her. You know I love my stories, but only very recently did they all start coming true."

"Aye, true enough," he said, grasping his wife's hand with a gleam in his eye that belied his love for her silly stories, notwithstanding.

"And if he's a Fomorian..."

"He could unite the kingdoms," she finished for me.

"The Goddess Brigid is Dagda's daughter, and as Joan guessed correctly, Bridget has her soul and her power. If Declan and Bridget stay together, they threaten his reign, mortal or not. Because as you've seen, the magic she possesses is nothing to scoff at.

"There are rituals that could be performed that could grant her immortality. Any high Fae could do it for her. And likely, many would once it was discovered who she was. Declan clinched it."

That one burned a little.

"If Declan and Bridget never met, then Bridget would have continued her life, never knowing her true power. Declan as well. No fairy would know their name unless they met them, except the elite. I've kept tabs on them as a part of my duty to the realm.

"It comes to my attention now because I think that this goes deeper than I anticipated. I think Dagda put it to the queen to take Bridget in exchange for Declan. It's a clever move by him, and the story fits.

"The queen would love nothing more than to have Declan, even grant him immortality. Under the guise of gunning for the crown, I almost didn't see the other elements at play.

"The queen is ambitious and fickle but rarely stupid. Facing Dagda even with the Fomorians would be more trouble than it was worth. No, I think Dagda needed her to do his dirty work so he could swoop in to save the day.

"He intends for Donn to immortalize Bridget so he could marry her to the Fomorian prince. Again.

"What prince?" Brian asked.

"Bres. Bres was Brigid's husband thousands of years ago, and it was their union that solidified Dagda's power. No supernatural creature would condone a Fomorian king; they're brutal and hated by their kind. But it's for that reason that peace must be kept with them.

"Bridget is the perfect way to do that, to allow the prince a say in council but no more power than that. Your son is Fomorian and the beloved Lugh; if he were to wed Bridget, he would be the next king of the Otherworld. Something Dagda wishes to prevent at all costs."

They were quiet for a moment before Brian said, "What happened to Brigid then?"

I swallowed hard.

"A story for another day," I replied.

Joan's look of sorrow told me everything.

"Now, take off the wardings. We're going to give them what they want."

CHAPTER 10

"That son of a bitch," I roared as I trashed another dresser.

Once the levy broke, there was no stopping it. By the time I had spent my rage, the room had been laid in pieces. Furniture overturned, mirrors smashed, four-post bed missing its posts, mattress askew.

All the while, the queen stood motionless. No alarm marked her features; she never moved to stop me, only maneuvering out of my path of destruction when necessary.

The wards were gone, and I was at her disposal. I was livid once again. And punched through a wall to slake the bloodthirst that ravaged me.

I wasn't sure I believed her, but the wards disappearing flicked that infernal switch that kept my simmering emotions at bay. Why would my mother remove the warding?

She would if Ruad told her to. But why?

If this was his play for Bridget's hand, it was a poor one. She wouldn't sit idly by and accept a man capable of such treachery unless she was a part of it.

The emotions eddied around me like ripples in a pond, rising and falling with every thought that raced through my mind. I sat in a pile of rubble, glass, and splintered wood that littered the floor. Leaning back against the wall that now bore the hole my fist put in it, I finally surveyed my shaking hands for damage.

Blood dripped in thick globs, running down my fingers, my forearms. Cuts decorated my hands and arms, and my knuckles were pummeled to oblivion.

And I loved it.

Yielding to the violence was like a drug. The pain and adrenaline the high. It was addicting and satisfying in a savage way. It was pure animal, no shred of humanity left. I felt like the heathen I was, underneath all of the social niceties thrust on me.

"Satisfying, I know," she rasped, cat eyes calm and assessing.

It was the most lucid I had ever seen her look. As if brutality were her normal state like she lived on the dark side.

I didn't deign to respond. She had won, and she knew it, but she wouldn't find an acquiescent subject in me, picking the glass and other debris out of my skin instead.

"You don't have to cage that side of you anymore," she murmured, edging closer to me with stalking strides.

I glared at her as I threw a piece of glass at her feet, red with my blood. She stopped her advance abruptly, the first hint of fear in her features.

She wasn't just treading lightly to avoid the rubble. Genuine panic shone in her eyes as she tried to survey the situation.

I took the opening she presented me. Stretching to my full height, I pounced, eating up the ground between us in three long strides.

"I don't have to?" I spat inches from her face, my voice hoarse with emotion.

And still, I strode forward. Her initial flinch had her backing away before I got closer, but now she peddled backward, hands behind her, blindly searching for something to ground herself with. When she finally found an overturned end table, I let out a harsh laugh before leaving her trembling in the demolished room.

I would feel bad if I didn't know she'd been goading me. If a reaction was what she wanted, I sure gave her one. Admittedly not the one she had desired, I thought bitterly.

Tearing down the sweeping staircase, I tried to figure out what to do now. The warding was gone. She should be able to manipulate me by now. Why wasn't she?

Unless she was...

But I never felt the cloying energy touch me unless she had made me forget. So many questions and no answers. The anger began to course through me, and I squeezed my hands into fists, the pain taking the edge off.

Pacing in front of the fire, I clenched and unclenched my hands, dripping blood on the floor with every step. Maybe it would push out whatever I had missed on my cursory cleansing.

Bridget wouldn't do that to me; she wouldn't double-cross me. I conjured images of her in her work clothes, talking animatedly with the customers. Her face was open and kind, listening to their woes and offering bits of her pain openly. Making sure they knew they weren't alone in their suffering or their triumph, buying dinners freely in celebration of the customer's latest news.

She was happy to buy things for her regulars out of her pocket. So glad to see them every week and hear about their days, listening attentively and remembering every detail no matter how insignificant. She lit up when the traveling customers made their way back to her after months of work elsewhere.

That wasn't the kind of duplicitous woman that the queen had described. I could see the sparkle in Bridget's eyes as she hugged a regular goodbye.

And I saw the toll it took on her at night. The dullness would settle on her features when it was all said and done. When she thought I wasn't looking and cleaned up the now empty room, and her shoulders would sag under the weight but never share the burden.

I always wondered what other burdens she shouldered. And whether she ever had someone to share them with.

She would go out with other men after the night was done or on her days off, but never one for long. And when we would go to her apartment after a long day, she was ready to dive into a show or a book.

Maybe a discussion about the table that always came in but never liked their meal. But personal stuff was only gleaned through passing comments and observations.

When she would cringe at specific comments, she withdrew herself smoothly from the conversation. And when she wouldn't flinch when the old chef had screamed in her face.

The way her eyes got distant when she was quiet. And how she would have an excuse not to see me that night. Leaving me to toss and turn in misery that night, reading until dusk shone on the horizon, wondering if she was alright.

Wondering if she was with someone.

Or the way her eyes shone the night we went out to eat instead of staying in and watching our shows. How she had let her hair down and had taken time with her makeup. The way she had twirled in front of me, asking if she looked okay in the outfit she had picked out.

She had looked remarkable. And the blush when I had said as much still heated my blood. I think I knew then what she meant to me, but I wasn't ready to admit it.

It was my idea to go out that night. I can't remember why but we had never discussed it. It was simply a fun idea. I knew I was attracted to her, but that night was different.

I had scowled at every man that looked at her twice. And there were more than a few. I'd taken every opportunity to get closer to her, place my hand on her waist, hold her hand.

But she needed things I wasn't ready to give. She deserved more than I could grant her.

144

And so I had left her at her apartment with our usual hug and kiss on the cheek. She had looked at me like she'd never seen the sunshine, and I was a ray of light.

She didn't look at Ruad like that. He hadn't been in the trenches with her like I had. Hadn't battled her demons with her.

So what's the angle, Ruad? You're no idiot. There has to be a play.

Somewhere in my reverie, I had stopped pacing and now stood staring at the wall of weapons. Gauntlets, daggers, and other weaponry glittered from the glow of the fire.

Stepping closer to examine a broad sword, the swirls in the steel a beautiful Damascus pattern like raindrops, I saw it. The pommel was a dark brown, insignificant from a distance. But up close, the dark brown was illuminated with the flames, and I saw that it wasn't opaque after all.

Inside that whiskey color was a dragonfly. And I knew I had my answer.

CHAPTER 11

Leaving Senan in charge of Brian and Joan again, I zapped myself off to Tech Duinn. Lesser fairies had to bother with the portal, but the Clurichaun, leprechaun, and High Fae like myself didn't need to.

And I was glad for it.

Traveling through cities like Tir Tairngire was like holding a court with the public. Everyone of every size and shape would bug me to get their voices heard—all clamoring to get what they wanted from Dagda and whomever else.

It wasn't that I avoided the public so much as I didn't have time to waste today. I frequented the local haunts like anybody else and my face wasn't uncommon in the city's streets. It may be more common than I would like to admit, but I didn't linger on that thought for long.

Tech Duinn didn't allow me much time to wallow, anyway. Like the city, the Underworld was a mass of energies, departed souls instead of living things but noisy all the same.

The cacophony hit me like a ton of bricks as energy swirled past me in every manner of disarray. Older souls, the weakened ones, were barely visible, wandering aimlessly around wondering how long until their rebirth. If they ever got one.

Newer souls were hardly different from their living forms. As boisterous in the afterlife as they'd been in life. Some were reincarnated immediately; others weren't as lucky.

Or unlucky, depending on your point of view.

The souls that were never reborn became ghosts and ghouls, haunting both realms. Assuming they had the energy to. If not, they were absorbed by the universe somehow. They were becoming plants and other lesser living things.

Life might be easier as a plant.

The cavernous room was muted in darkness. Inky blackness weaved through every nook and cranny of the cave mouth, lending to the grim atmosphere.

The hustle and bustle were exactly like the life they had lived. Souls reliving portions of their lives on repeat, eating food that wasn't there, talking to people I couldn't see. Some broke free from the monotony; the longer you were there, the more likely one would awaken from the trance.

Those were the ones to awaken others and torture them usually. The one's no longer welcome topside.

Like Carman and her sons.

Gratefully I didn't recognize anyone near me right now. But that didn't mean that they didn't know me.

Even if I couldn't pick out a face in the crowd, it didn't mean that I wasn't personally responsible for their residence here. It was a long life I had lived and a brutal one.

There had been many wars to preserve Dagda's throne, and I would gladly fight them again even if I weren't thrilled with him lately. But just as the queen would leave a power vacuum, so would Dagda, and he was better suited to the position than anyone else. Currently.

Any cognizant being here that knew my face was sure to spread the word quickly. They had little else to occupy the time with.

And then trouble would ensue.

If not for my crimes, then for those of Dagda. No good ruler didn't make enemies. No ruler didn't make enemies, period, but the opposition of a just ruler was the scourge of civilized society. And many were headed my way now.

Making the most of the time I had, I careened through the open space, headed toward the tunnel where Bridget would be. It wasn't difficult to find, the sable hole like a gaping wound, drawing your attention with its ghastliness.

No sentinels guarded the entrance to the heart of Tech Duinn; the God of Death needed no warriors. He took as he pleased.

The fear that should have shivered down my spine was a shaft of steel. A man with nothing to lose was feared, and I was that man.

I had made it barely past the maw of that great passage before I was knocked to the ground by something large and solid. The darkness obscured my vision more than the lack of oxygen to my lungs, as I lay there floundering for air.

"The right-hand man so quickly dispatched? You must be joking, Ruad," a gravelly voice said from a distance.

A pale face hovered above me momentarily before I was lifted off of the ground and onto my feet in one fell swoop. The body that accompanied the face was Fomorian, and distant bells rang in my head with recognition.

"Bres," I spat.

Brigid's husband.

His answering sneer told me he knew who was responsible for his demise. The smile that crept across my face was pure satisfaction.

"Finished?" that husky voice rang out again.

"Quite," I sniped as I turned my attention to Donn.

His sable hair fell to his shoulders in stringy waves, face pale, thin lips pressed in an unamused line. The God of Death was unimpressive if it weren't for those eyes that stared back at me through his sickly features.

There was no distinguishing between the pupils and irises; both were an unfathomable black like the tunnel we were now in. They seemed to swallow any light or happiness that dared enter his presence.

Despite myself, a chill raced down my spine at those eyes, gazing straight to the heart of me. Though I knew nothing showed, I saw the flicker resonate in those eyes as he picked up on my innermost thoughts.

He leaned forward in his chair, a monstrosity of a thing. Solid black marble cleaved from the cave in which we stood, intricately carved with scenes of horror even I blanched at.

"Is she really worth all the hassle?" he asked at last.

"Yes," I breathed.

Bres snickered beside me, muttering something off-color about her that I refused to hear; it took all of my quiet reserve not to take the bait. This was bigger than him or me.

Donn seemed to be weighing my heart like the Egyptian God Anubis. Determining my worthiness.

He was quiet for long moments. As I waited with bated breath, I saw the wheels churning behind those eyes. Whatever he saw in mine had him leaning back in his grotesque chair.

I made my plans abundantly apparent, speaking to whatever strange power the old God possessed. Like a lover's caress, his magic slid over my skin, probing beneath the surface to uncover what lay beneath. It was dark and seductive, and I could imagine allowing that embrace to swallow me whole, never fighting its siren song.

The wicked gleam in his eye when his power returned to him was answer enough.

CHAPTER 12

I felt her presence behind me, an infection in the room. She emanated a wildness with every heartbeat that echoed in the silence, and I vaguely wondered why I was able to hear it.

"Why?" I asked her without turning around.

I wanted her to talk more than I wanted an answer. Something to keep her engaged, so she didn't notice that the wards were gone. If she hadn't noticed already.

"We want to deal with mortals again. Like the fly is eaten by the fish, which is then eaten by the bear, the universe has designed Fae and humans to fit into the delicate ecosystem."

"And then the bear is killed by a human, who is in turn killed by a Fae," I said dully.

"Mmm killed or otherwise," she said with enthusiasm.

That tone was why I wanted to keep her talking. To keep my *word* to Bridget.

"But what's to gain? You're not hurting from the lack." I gestured to the grandeur of the room without so much as a glance her way.

"Like you humans were content with the little magic we had given you? The technology we helped you with? No, you needed more. All creatures are that way."

"What more can we give you?"

"Everything." Her breathless reply made me turn at last.

I raised my eyebrows in silent question, urging her to elaborate.

She wasn't facing me to see it, but she continued on all the same. She slowly made her way to the couch, dragging a painted black fingernail along the back of it as she walked.

"Different Fae have different abilities, and the lesser are more likely to eat you. But some of the more powerful require human sacrifices for their power."

"Like you," I supplied.

"Mmm like me indeed." Her eyes flashed with desire, and she ran a hand idly on her thigh, her dress hitching up as she did so.

I averted my attention to the fire as she laughed low and husky. But it gave me the impression that the power she craved would have to be from a willing participant.

All fairy power usually came with stipulations, and I hope she just gave away hers.

"So what have you done in the absence of your preferred prey?"

"Lesser fairies accomplish the goal to an extent. But they know what they're signing up for. It takes some of the excitement out of it if you ask me."

"But not every fairy needs to sacrifice for power," I commented.

She studied me for a moment before responding, picking at her nails as she did so.

"There are many different forms of power," she began, "but no, not always. Some do, as you humans must eat to live; some fairies do as well. However, others merely enjoy the thrill that accompanies gaining power in such a manner."

"Like you," I repeated.

Her eyes flashed malevolently as a smile curved those sinister lips. It was answer enough.

"Now, have you quite finished your interrogation?" she remarked lazily as if I was boring her.

I made a guttural noise in response—something between not really and whatever, turning to the fireplace again to avoid her.

"You never asked the most pressing question, Declan. One might misconstrue that to mean that you didn't care about the welfare of your beloved." She clicked her tongue at that one, a mocking admonishment.

Proof enough that she knew I was in control of my faculties. I didn't think my overreaction upstairs helped my case. Oh well.

"If you knew, why didn't you do anything?" I asked.

I'd never felt the telltale tingle of power that she was attempting to manipulate me. And I wasn't sure what to think about that.

"If I knew," she scoffed. "If you were trying to pretend otherwise, you did a piss-poor job.

"Nonetheless, my knowledge of your scheming and subsequent loss of protection is irrelevant. You're not for me."

"Then who am I for?"

She smirked at me.

"Your good friend hasn't told you yet?"

"Enough of that, get to the point."

Rolling her eyes, she sat further up on the couch.

"I wonder if he's figured it out or not. But there is another way your power can serve me better.

"Not as a payment to Donn, no, that would be a waste of your *talents.* Rather as my husband will you *serve me* best."

"Good luck," I scoffed.

"Oh, luck has little to do with it. You placed your wards thinking it could prevent me from controlling you, but I don't need to lift a finger so long as we hold Bridget."

I kept my breathing as even as possible, but the tightening in my chest was involuntary.

"What you didn't know perhaps was that she's not your Bridget to save anymore. Dagda has plans far greater for her than for her to shack up with a Fomorian bastard like you."

Fomorian? I was trying and failing to follow the conversation, but I knew I didn't like where it was going.

"What about Bridget?" I asked reluctantly.

She wanted to get a rise out of me again, but I wouldn't give her the satisfaction a second time. Losing my temper was a mistake I wouldn't make again.

"Aw, there it is," she taunted me. "Your eyes go all soft when you say her name."

I growled, but she didn't flinch. Instead, she rose from her seat to stand by the fire, looking into the flames instead of at me.

"I might even pity you. The two of you sots. What is it about her that makes you both whine so damn much? She's gone, and you both climb into the bottom of a bottle and wait for her to come back."

My hands clenched into fists again, and the ache wasn't as unbearable as it should've been. Maybe the adrenaline spiking my veins kept the agony at bay. I wouldn't chance a glance at them before her soliloquy was through, but she knew how to push my buttons. A fact evident on her blood-red lips quirking up in amusement.

"Normally, I'd find this behavior pathetic. In some ways, I still do—what a monstrous vulnerability from two formidable warriors. That right there is why I might pity you. How ruthless you each would be if not for her. It's a shame. That's why I keep my life unattached. Simpler that way.

"But I would be remiss not to note the balance she brings to your lives. Isn't that always the way of things? You'd be unstoppable if not for her. And that might be the beauty of it all. No world could contain a brute like you, but she makes you malleable.

"Fortunate for her father and me. How we could wield you both with her. Like arrows in need of a bow. Capable of so much and yet rendered useless without your string. Your effectiveness is dependent upon the wielder.

"But the best leaders know that wars are often not won on battlefields but behind closed doors. To win, you have to dismantle the opposition before they have the chance to build. So many of your human wars could have been prevented had someone had the foresight to stomp the seeds of dissent before they sprouted.

"It's not chance the three of you have been scattered like seeds in the wind. Together you are the forest, and apart, you wither without the environment to survive."

"Are you nearing the conclusion of your diatribe?"

She sent a scalding glance my way, throwing her dark hair over a shoulder. A look a lesser man would have shied from. Or a smarter one.

"You would do well to mind your tongue, boy," she seethed. "Cocksure doesn't equate to much in this realm; the sweetest fairy is likely the one that will eat you alive. And the angriest will grind your bones to make the bread for their breakfast all the same."

I was past tired of her incessant rambling and gave her a wave of acknowledgment to continue. In the nicest way I could muster, that is.

"Your insolence aside, you are valuable, and I am nearing the end of my spiel. I'd have been finished without your interruption."

It took a great deal of effort not to roll my eyes. I likely would have if she weren't looking pointedly at me.

"The point is that there are those that find your alliance threatening—Fae scarier than myself. So it would be in your best interest to stay with me, to protect Bridget. If you continue to associate with the two of them, you will never be able to rest.

154

"Threats will be ever-present in your lives. And how would that be for your precious pet? She has been through so much already. Surely you wouldn't want to be the one to cause her more suffering?"

She finished the last and let it linger between us. As the silence stretched, I saw the validity of her words and the trap. Her explanation was self-serving, but was there no truth in it?

I'd never experienced supernatural beings before Bridget, and neither had she. However, changing tactics from "Bridget planned this" to "poor Bridget" was suspicious as best.

"You didn't get to the point," I observed.

Now it was her turn to roll her eyes. And she did so with dramatic flair.

"Bridget is in the Underworld. Being prepared to be reincarnated as the full-fledged Goddess she favors."

"Why?"

"To do her duty to the realm."

I had an idea what that meant, and I didn't like it. Also, I was pretty sure Bridget's family wouldn't be my biggest fans.

CHAPTER 13

I grabbed the Serch Bythol in my hand, asking it for an answer.

Just because it worked for Declan didn't mean it didn't work for me too. It wasn't a fact I felt necessary to rub in for Declan.

I'd had my own for centuries, and it was the first indicator I had when Brigid made another resurgence. Thousands of years, it had been silent, the chain the ancient symbol sat upon a heavy weight to remind me.

The time for remembering was over.

Nothing had changed yet, but the dragonfly in the hilt of my sword promised me that everything soon would.

Finally.

Donn had promised me he would honor my wishes, and I had promised him that I knew the cost. Dealing with the Devil himself left a foul taste in my mouth, but desperate times called for desperate measures.

The pendant in my hand lay silent and foreboding, and I tried not to wait patiently. I couldn't risk Dagda catching wind of my plans, so I had told Senan alone what I had in mind as I released the wards on the house.

We had taken Declan's parents home and placed the protection around them instead, with only promises that all would be well if a little different from what we had planned.

Joan had given me a knowing look. She may not know, but her intuition told her something was up, and I meant what I said.

We'd left Declan's prone form unprotected, the only trouble with my plan. I didn't think the queen would question her good fortune though.

It would be very different, but it was the only way out of this mess that I saw.

Brian had looked only at his wife before giving me a nod, trusting her gut more than his own. The suspicion continued to shine in his eyes, but he knew better than to deny her feelings.

I'd gone back to my residence in the Otherworld, a quiet cottage in the countryside. I wanted to be at peace before there wasn't any left.

Well, before there wasn't any left for me.

It was then that I felt it, while I drank tea at the breakfast nook. Like butterflies in my stomach, and I went to go meet Brigid again.

Keep Reading

Fireflies is available at major retailers.

You have just read Dragonflies.

Butterflies Launch To Be Determined

Follow Me

Join My Weekly Newsletter

https://sheahulse13.com